REVOLT

RAY BOURHIS

ISBN 979-8-9944867-0-2 (Paperback)
ISBN 979-8-9944867-1-9 (eBook)

Printed in United States

ACKNOWLEDGMENTS

Thanks go to Debby Phillips, Ann Marie Do, Tony Coyne, Moira Buxbaum, and Suzanne McCafferty, for their invaluable editing and technical assistance.

And to Danielle, Matthew, Bobby, and Andrew Bourhis for their insights, support, inspiration and patience.

CONTENTS

PROLOGUE

Excessive taxes and oppressive regulation, uncontrolled budget deficits and crooked CEOs, price-gouging oil companies and fat-cat lobbyists, automated phone menus and torturous hold music, Monsanto and Equifax, lying insurance companies and corrupt politicians... there is no end to it. No end to the hideous and the obnoxious, the frustrating and the disgusting.

But try to do something about it? Try to fight back in any way beyond sending a meaningless email to a feckless public relations clerk in some Call Center in the middle of Dogpatch, USA, and you might just learn why it would have been a good deal smarter and a whole lot safer to have just bitten your tongue and kept your big mouth shut.

INTRODUCTION

The first time I met him, he made a lasting impression. He looked like a retired bouncer out of some cheap Reno cowboy bar equipped with smelly leatherette barstools and slot machines in the bathroom.

Wearing a faded green polo shirt tucked tightly into a pair of Wrangler jeans, he introduced himself as "Mister" Brontel as he handed me a dog-eared business card. He had an expression on his face like the cop I'd met up with years before, standing over a ticking parking meter, citation book in hand, waiting for it to expire.

Having never been audited before, I was a bit taken aback by Brontel. Frankly, I'd expected more of an IRS agent. As months and years flew by, and the audit continued, my take on him grew worse and worse as he poured over page after page of Visa and MasterCard records, telephone bills, stock-portfolio statements, check registers, and bank statements. On and on and on. The more he read, the more questions he had. Not just about financial and tax records, but about other things as well. Although his questions were always asked in the context of audit issues, such as "What was the business purpose of this April trip to New York" or "Who was the person you called at this telephone number that you wrote off as a business expense," as time went on it became increasingly clear that the purpose of my IRS audit was not limited solely to tax matters. The

IRS knew things it could not have known unless it had read my emails and listened in on my phone conversations.

Finally, when Mr. Brontel asked for copies of the rough drafts of manuscripts I was in the midst of writing (about corporate crime and payoffs to politicians disguised as campaign contributions), I decided I'd had enough. I called him a sleazy hack and ordered him out of my office. Not long thereafter, I received a letter demanding that I pay the IRS more than $43,000 as a result of supposedly improper deductions revealed in its audit. I went to a tax lawyer who said I would have to pay a $10,000 retainer, and that my representation would likely cost at least three or four times that amount just to appeal the audit findings to the level of an IRS supervisor. Then, the attorney added, the supervisor would most likely uphold the auditor's findings, and if I wanted to challenge that, I would have to go to tax court at a cost of tens of thousands of dollars more. "Most people," he said sadly, "just give up, and pay the devil his due."

Why me? I thought. *And what about their knowing stuff from my writings and emails?*

Then it happened. I woke up to a headline in the *New York Times*: "IRS Targeting Political Groups for Audits." Soon the story was all over the country. The IRS was collecting information on and harassing individuals and groups based on their political beliefs. All kinds of individuals and organizations. Both on the Right and on the Left. It wasn't just me! What was the government doing? What was going on here? Was the Country, MY Country, compiling dossiers on its own people? Was it invading the privacy of its citizens—tapping into phone conversations? Reading correspondence? Intimidating law-abiding citizens? All in the name of what? National Security?

Had it really come to that?

CHAPTER ONE

NUTSS

Sean Cogan stood there, looking like a cross between a sweet humored baby-faced Paul Rudd and a scrappy, rugged Russell Crow. Wearing a five-hundred dollar T- shirt from Wilkes Bashford and a pair of frayed eight year old chinos from God knows where, he was nursing a Pinot Grigio as he watched dozens of guests, many of whom were old friends, nibbling on brochette and grilled artichoke hearts. He was trying to look matter-of-factish, but the expression on his face gave a new meaning to "uh-oh." No doubt about it. He was up to something.

The overflow crowd had come out to raise money for Neighbors United to Save Squirrels (NUTSS), an organization formed to protect a newly discovered colony of endangered red-tailed squirrels living in Oak Tree Canyon, and doing their best to survive the fallout from the developers who had descended on Fairview years before.

In addition to the usual locals, the crowd included some folks Sean didn't recognize. Women with expensive tattoos sporting exotic jewelry and men in designer jeans. They were out en-masse, checkbooks in hand, ready to do their part for the environment.

Following an impassioned presentation by a renowned mammologist from Earth First's Tamiasciurus Project—a presentation complete with squirrel population charts, lagomorph studies, survival curves, and *Save*

The Red Tail bumper stickers—the crowd milled around. Cogan had waited for the right moment. "David, I've given a lot of thought to this. We can't just stand around letting this happen…"

David Oster had the mind, appearance, and disposition of a CPA, which was exactly what he was. Prematurely graying and prematurely predictable, he was a big fan of Cogan—his temperamental antithesis.

"What are you talking about?" he replied with a mouthful of cashews, his mind obviously still riveted on squirrels. "What's going on? What's… "

"The government's corrupt," Cogan interrupted. "The American Republic is dead, sold to the highest bidder." From across the room, looking in their direction but just out of earshot, stood Jen Renton. She too had known Cogan since high school, when he wouldn't give her the time of day. But now… things might be different.

"We've got to do something, David. We can't just sit around. We're fiddling while Paris burns."

"Rome," replied David, who had switched from nuts to Camembert on a cracker.

"What?"

"While Rome burns, not Paris."

"Rome. Paris. Fresno. I don't give a shit."

David, Cogan's oldest friend, had heard it all before. His response was predictable.

"You're a little off the deep end on this stuff. We've been over this many times. And besides, you can't do anything about it. Nobody can do anything about it. You of all people know that. The system is what it is…"

Cogan cut him off.

"We HAVE to change it. This has been going on for far too long. We're not getting any younger, David. We owe it to future generations. How long can we just continue to wait? We have to put a stop to it."

"What can we do? Nothing. It's just the way it is." It was the wrong thing to say.

"Don't be an idiot," Cogan snapped. "Don't be a fucking robot."

"C'mon Sean. Ease up."

Cogan fixed a steady gaze on his friend. He took a deep breath and let it out slowly. "It's not about easing up, David. It's about doing exactly the opposite. It's about shaking things up." "What do you mean?"

"We need to say NO. Refuse to continue playing the game. Refuse to be a part of it anymore."

"What are you talking about? Refuse to be a part of what?"

"Refuse to be a part of the system. We need to set our own standards. To make our own rules. To have a government accountable to us, not to the lobbyists and billionaires who run things in Washington."

"How?"

Sean paused. "By putting an initiative on the ballot—right here, in Fairview, declaring our independence. Our independence from everything their payoffs have created."

"We can't do that. You're talking about laws, court decisions… How can we just not abide by the law?"

"That's what the whole civil rights movement was about. That's what any resistance movement is about. That's what ignoring the Supreme Court's <u>Dred</u> <u>Scott</u> decision was about. It was about people saying 'No, we're not going to abide by these rules anymore'."

Suddenly the space surrounding David and Sean fell so quiet it was as though they were under water. David's cracker froze in mid-air. He searched for a smile, a grin, even a smirk. Something, anything, to signal this was just a joke. Sean gave him nothing.

"Sean, you must be kidding. You can't do that," blustered David. "It's probably illegal…"

Cogan forged ahead, his voice rising "I already looked up the initiative process. It's in the elections code," he said. "All you have to do to put something on the ballot is to write it up, walk into the town clerk's office, pay two hundred and fifty bucks, file it, and start collecting signatures. When you get the required number, it goes on the ballot. This November is perfect. The only other thing people will be voting on is the town council."

"Sean, you're not serious." The cracker was all but forgotten.

"I'm damn serious. I'm going to file it tomorrow. Nobody's going to jail. We're talking about voting. Simply voting."

"You're out of your mind."

Cogan shrugged. Out of the corner of his eye, he noticed Jen Renton coming over to join the conversation. The brilliant high school geek he'd ignored had grown up to be tall and sultry. How could he have known? Following graduation, she'd gone on to Boston University, then to law school in New Mexico. She'd worked as a corporate litigator for a dozen years with some staid Albuquerque law firm, and then she just bailed. Cutthroat big business litigation had burned her out. She had grown too close to the corporate world for her own ethical comfort. She quit practicing law and moved back to Fairview to study shiatsu and become a massage therapist.

As she drew closer, Cogan berated himself for all the times he had blown her off. No more the gangly geek from her high school days, she was a knockout. Now she delighted in getting Cogan back for ignoring her when they were teenagers.

"Hi guys. How's the Camembert?"

"Jen," David asked, ignoring the question, "what would you say if I told you Sean wants to put an initiative on the November ballot for Fairview to declare its independence. Basically to ignore any higher authority?"

Jen tilted her head. "A vote to set our own standards? To refuse to be bound by congressional and court-made decisions that we disagree with? A page from the civil disobedience manual?"

"That's exactly what I mean," Sean nodded. "The people of Fairview could take a vote on any important issue. And if the town voted for or against something we would respond accordingly. Only, unlike most civil disobedience, this would have the official stamp of approval of our entire town."

A grin crossed Jennifer's face as the idea sunk in. She started to giggle.

Jen had always been a closet revolutionary. But having lawyered for years on behalf of the oil, pharmaceutical, and chemical companies of the world gave her plenty of reasons to come out. "For Fairview to become independent? With our own laws?"

"Right."

"Could we write our own Constitution? Have our own courts? Appoint our own judges?"

Cogan thought about Jen's legal background. "I guess that's right."

Jen's face lit up. Her eyes widened. She was clearly warming to the idea. "Refusing to go along with Big Brother's rules?"

"Exactly."

Jen pondered for a few seconds.

"OK. Count me in," she said. "What can I do?"

"Can you do some legal research?" Cogan asked.

"You bet." Jen smiled as she grabbed David's Camembert and popped it in her mouth.

David was incredulous. "You're crazy... You're both crazy."

"Let's take a little poll," Cogan said. "Let's see if there are any other crazies here." He started to work the room, Jen and David in tow. Fairview residents were known to be an eccentric lot, and the cross section of them at this particular fundraiser was even more so. Pretty soon the place started to buzz with snickering excitement. The decibel level increased as disagreements erupted.

"OK. Let's give it the acid test. Where's Ollie?"

Ollie Waterson, also a former classmate, was Cogan's political polar opposite. His truck, a classic Humvee, was awash in bumper stickers proclaiming the rights of gun owners and the evils of abortion. Waterson's favorite, *Evolution is Horse Shit*, sat right in the center next to a decal of a smirking tea-cup. Cogan found him in the kitchen, waving a bottle of Chianti and chatting up a caterer half his age over a bowl of carrot sticks.

"Ollie," Cogan demanded, interrupting a pickup line, "listen up. What would you say about the idea of placing an initiative on the ballot for

Fairview to declare its independence and, basically, to ignore laws from higher authorities that it disagreed with. To make its own rules?" Ollie studied Cogan's face.

"C'mon Sean, I don't have time for this." The reason was obvious. Cogan didn't blink, staring straight ahead as he waited. Finally, Ollie couldn't resist. "Are you serious?" He cast a dubious glance at Jen and David.

"Completely," replied Cogan. "The whole damn system has been corrupted to the core. Big money. Big government. Big labor. Big corporations. Big everything. Millions and billions and trillions of dollars running the whole show. Of, by, and for the people is as dead as the Founding Fathers."

"And you want to change all of that with a Fairview initiative?"

"No. That's the problem. We could never change it. The big guys have the power; we don't. They have the money; we don't. They own the politicians; we don't. They control the print and broadcast media; we don't. They appoint the judges; we don't. We can't defeat them. The only thing we can do is to declare that we've had it. That we aren't going play their game anymore."

"With an initiative?"

"Absolutely," Cogan said. "I'm talking about putting it right on the damn ballot this coming November."

"But you just said they can crush any initiative with their money."

"Big statewide initiatives, yes. But that won't do them any good in a local election.

The more they spend, the more they'll be proving our point."

A sly grin came over Ollie's face. "Could we have our own Treasury Department? Our own Federal Reserve? Our own currency? Our own Justice Department? Could we go back to the gold standard?"

"Why not? We could certainly vote on it."

"What about taxes? Could we dump the income tax and just have a sales tax?"

"That would be ok with me."

David was standing there with his mouth open.

"A balanced budget requirement?"

"Absolutely. Deficit spending has everyone going crazy. It's insane."

"Inheritance taxes?"

"Who needs 'em?"

Ollie's eyes suddenly grew to twice their normal size. "Wait a minute," he said, "Why couldn't Fairview become an independent tax haven – like the Turks and Caicos," he smiled. An off-shore – on shore banking center, like with Lichtenstein. Or the Island of Jersey?

Ha. What an IRS kick in the ass that would be! Money would fly in here from all over. From Silicon Valley, from Hollywood, from the VC firms, from the money managers. Have you ever seen the names on the building directories in the Caribbian? They'd all be setting up profit centers here to avoid taxes – for fat fees. And now that places like Switzerland have agreed to share deposit information with the US, if we refused to do that, all that business would come to us." Ollie's eyes were glistening like gold nuggets. "Ok," he said, "I'm in."

"Ollie, you can't be serious?" David couldn't believe it. His face contorted into a pained expression of absolute incredulity.

"Damn right," Ollie said, working himself up on the spot. "I'm fed up with all the crap. All these politicians—Democrats, Republicans, all of them—just running around with their hands out. I'm sick of it. Really sick of it.

"In fact, I'll work on the damn initiative if you want me to. I'm a strict constructionist, as you know. The revolutionaries: Payne, Jefferson, Paul Revere. They had it right. Limited government. Accountable to the people. They would roll over in their graves to see how the corrupt windbags running things these days operate. It's time we got back to small government. Back to the people being in charge instead of big business and its goddamned bagmen. And I'll tell you who else had it right. Teddy Roosevelt."

"The trust buster," Cogan nodded.

"I consider myself more of a bust truster," Ollie snorted. "Anyway, it's time to send the super-rich some shock waves. To raise a little hell."

Danielle Hall, a savvy, strong woman, who looked like she was spending a lot of time spinning at the gym, had migrated to the kitchen to hear Ollie's take on the idea. She was a senior accounts manager for a big public relations firm. Her day job involved a different kind of spinning—turning corporate disasters into positive news stories. If a securities firm was caught churning client accounts or flipping IPOs, Danielle would write the press releases and full-page newspaper ads comparing the company's track record to the S&P 500.

"Count on me," she said, without explanation. And so it went. One conversation after the next. Soon folks were volunteering to help gather signatures to qualify an initiative for the November ballot.

"Apparently squirrel lovers and revolutionaries have something in common," joked Cogan. The more the conversation spread and the more the wine flowed, the more enthusiastic the crowd became. Finally, Carl Sandgrow couldn't take it anymore.

Carl, a thin, dignified veteran of a long line of Fairview political campaigns, owned the local hardware store. It had been in his family for two or three generations and had survived fires, floods, and what Carl sneeringly referred to as the invasion of Bozo-Walton and his Walmart Big Top. Carl was a man of few words. He stood alone, his frail left hand grasping the back of a folding chair, looking every bit the solitary portrait of an aging Mr. Roberts having arrived in the belly of the beast. He cleared his throat.

"I hope," Carl began, "that all of you are having a good time with this screwball idea. But before you write this thing up and march on down to town hall, you'd better think long and hard about the repercussions. Regardless of what happens, for a town like ours to even be considering what amounts to a vote of no confidence – in our leaders, in our system— will attract a hell of a lot of attention. It will look bad—really bad—for

Fairview and for the whole country. You will be accused of giving aid and comfort to our enemies and encouragement to loose cannons and tinhorn dictators all over. America haters and capitalism bashers will use this to turn the U.S. into a laughing stock. This will wind up on television, in the papers, on the Internet… Self-appointed patriots will respond. As they always do. They will go after anyone behind this with a vengeance."

"Are you serious?" said Cogan."

"You're damn right," Carl replied. "You're going to be dealing with every big hat on Wall Street and in Washington—and all of their buddies. Big oil, big banks, big insurance, big drug companies, big defense contractors, big manufacturers, big securities dealers, big everything. These guys don't fool around. They're not just going to sit around and let a bunch of wine and cheese swillers from Fairview make them look like a gaggle of flying asses. Do not do this."

Cogan looked around. Blank faces had suddenly turned serious. Friends he had known for years were glancing furtively away in nervous silence. Were they scared? Were they afraid to simply stand up on their two feet and tell big business and their politician puppets to go to hell?

Cogan broke the silence "You know what, Carl?" he replied, a touch of aggravation in his voice, "You're probably right. But that just demonstrates the problem. That's what our country has become."

Making eye contact with David, he continued. "That's why instead of running and hiding, we have to do this. We can't allow what is going on to continue. Look at us. We're afraid of our own system, our own so-called leaders, and our own government. That is wrong! It can't continue. We have to make a statement. Loud and clear. We have to tell them to go to hell. That we have had it. That the people of Fairview may not have the power to change things but that doesn't mean we want to continue to be a part of it.

"We may lose. We may make fools of ourselves. We may be called horrible names. We may be vilified, demonized, humiliated, and God knows what else. For what? For voting our distain and contempt for what has happened to our Country? People say there should be democracy in Iraq, in Afghanistan, in Syria, in Somalia, in Egypt, in Saudi Arabia, in China. That people should have the right to vote, without fear, for whomever and whatever they want.

I say let's have some of that right here in Fairview. Let's see what the people think." Some shuffled around nervously, as though they just wanted to get back to saving squirrels. Others acted as though somebody had suddenly flipped a switch inside their heads; their eyes were bright and their faces animated. "Are you with me?" he asked. Supporters cheered. Hooting and whistling filled the air as years of pent-up frustration erupted. Carl Sandgrow didn't even bother responding. Cogan, looking like he was waking from a dream, just smiled. He caught Jen's eye. She was smiling too.

In a darkened corner of the room a short, neatly dressed, middle-aged man pulled a cellphone from his pocket and strolled out onto a balcony overlooking a stand of trees. The expression on his face left little doubt as to the seriousness of the call he was placing. Silently, he began to dial.

It was Monday, August 10. Cogan woke up early and put up a pot of coffee. After rummaging around for a note pad, he sat down at his kitchen table and started to write. Three cups and several drafts later, he was done. Holding it up to the light, he read:

PROPOSITION A

The Town of Fairview, in order to establish a government of by and for its people, hereby declares its independence from any and all other government entities of any kind whatsoever; and reserves unto itself the right to reject any laws, regulations or rulings from others which, by majority vote of Fairview's citizens, it deems to be unjust, unfair or immoral.

Yes _______ No _______

Cogan drove down to town hall, plunked down the two-hundred-fifty-dollar fee, and handed the initiative to the disheveled desk clerk. She read it, her eyes widened, and she read it again. She stared at Cogan, shook her head, and muttered something under her breath. She placed the paper on her desk and retreated to a far corner of the office to fuss with permit applications.

Outside, Cogan got on his cellphone and started dialing. It was the morning after and all that. Sean's friends had busy lives. Families, careers, obligations, commitments. Were they still interested? Were they serious about it? It was okay, Cogan explained to each, if they wanted to take a pass. And it would certainly be a good idea to think about it very seriously before jumping in with both feet. The whole thing could well wind up as a big embarrassment. It could be hard later on to explain their involvement. On the one hand, it might not even get off the ground. They might not be able to get the necessary signatures and so on. On the other hand, it could spin totally out of control. It could become a big deal. Very time consuming. Very unpredictable. Nobody should feel any obligation to proceed. But they would have nothing of his offer.

It was unanimous. Nobody wanted out. All of them still gravitated to the places they'd hung out as kids, and they decided to meet in two days, on August 12, at the Depot.

CHAPTER TWO

THE DEPOT

The Book Depot, long a local landmark, was housed in Fairview's old Railway station. Like most train service in the United States, the rail line was cut back in the 1950s to rid communities of the "noise pollution" created by ding-donging wigwags and clickety-clacking train cars, all as part of the oil industry's grand campaign for the environment.

The former passenger station now housed a café and an old-fashioned bookstore, which in addition to the requisite collection of bestsellers carried an impressive array of regional hiking and biking books, foreign and out-of-state newspapers, travel magazines, and poetry. A faded beige wall featuring the works of local artists separated the bookstore section from ten or twelve tables that overlooked the town square and its surrounding storefront boutiques and restaurants.

Sean, Jen, Ollie, and Danielle were joined by Geoffrey Santorum, the owner of The Book Depot. Geoffrey had gone to school with the rest of them and had taken over The Depot when its founders, his eccentric parents, retired. Geoffrey was a lover of books and a successful ghostwriter for several famous novelists. His ghostwriting made it possible to keep The Depot open. He also taught tai quan do twice a week at the Y.

They sat huddled in a corner nursing lattes and cups of tea, feeling vaguely conspiratorial about what they were discussing. Danielle, because of her job, had a ton of experience dealing with the print and broadcast world and their aggressive approach to collecting news as sound bites. She would handle the media side of things. "What's happened to our country is incredible," she said. "Our freedom, our independence, our privacy have all been taken away."

"Despite higher and higher taxes, the futures of our children and grandchildren continue to be sacrificed on the altar of out-of-control deficit spending," added Ollie. "And with the government debt we are incurring, future generations will never see it paid off."

"The more people realize the extent of what is going on, the more pissed off they get," Danielle continued. "This isn't a liberal versus conservative thing. It's not about Republicans versus Democrats. A lot of folks—of all stripes—have just really had it. They just don't know what they can do about it."

"Until now," Cogan said. "Jen, I really need you to do some hard legal research on the whole independence issue. That has got to be really complicated. And we want what we're doing to be a credible statement. Not like a civil insurrection, but more like a maybe-smaller-is-better bloodless experiment. A formal statement from a small town in America explaining that things have gotten so bad they won't blindly go along anymore "

"I already started," Jen replied. "There are all kinds of different examples of recent past and current independence movements going on all over the world. All in an effort to secure greater governmental accountability, express frustration with corruption and secure more local autonomy from outside control. In addition to obvious examples like Quebec, Scotland, Ukraine, Hong Kong, Tibet, Taiwan, and the Baltics, you also have islands all over the Caribbean, the South Pacific, Micronesia, even in Europe. Some have wound up securing their own self rule, their own governments. Others have remained loosely affiliated with other countries—France, England, or the U.S. There are also tiny places like Lichtenstein, Monaco, even the Vatican, which though physically attached to

France or Italy or Austria nevertheless operate as quasi-separate entities. In the U.S. you have the independent or semi-independent Native American reservations. Plus scattered movements within existing states. What would be different in what we are doing here is that rarely, if ever, has a political entity, such as a town, actually voted to secure its autonomy. That's as far as I've gotten."

"Interesting. Geoffrey, Ollie, can you start in on the political side? We need to know how many signatures we have to get. How much time do we have to get them? What's the voter profile in this town? How do we keep this whole thing mainstream? What do we need to do to keep it rational, organized, under control?"

The group talked about setting up a loosely defined coordinating apparatus. Their efforts had to be well organized. Danielle emphasized the need to take a very mainstream approach. "No wild demonstrations," she suggested. "Nobody parading around in a Ben Franklin costume."

Cogan wasn't so sure. "We need all the free press we can get. I was actually thinking of bringing in the Sisters of Perpetual Indulgence to help launch our petition drive with one of their naked benedictions." Cogan's idea was met with stunned silence.

"Have you ever seen these folks in action? Their leader is called the Nun of the Above. She wears this tiny miniskirt with a black and white hooded veil and a sheer, lacy camisole. It's very sexy. The papers would gobble it up." For several seconds everyone except Cogan sat there fidgeting. Finally, mercifully, with a huge grin, he broke the chill.

"Gotcha," he laughed.

As the meeting ended, the same guy who had placed the cellphone call at the NUTTS fundraiser gathered his papers off the nearby table, removed his earphones, and prepared to pay his bill. To all but the most sophisticated techno geek, his headset looked identical to the earbuds you always see connected to iPods. But that wasn't what they were. Joseph Iverson's earphones and wires were used for a very different purpose than listening to music. Iverson was going to be having a busy evening. Some things would have to wait until tomorrow, though. It was already close to 6 pm in central Texas.

The next day, Cogan drove to Peet's for his morning coffee. Half of Fairview went to Peet's every morning to wake up with cappuccinos, espressos, lattés, mochas, a dozen kinds of teas—even plain old coffee. Peet's featured sofas, easy chairs and the latest local and national newspapers.

Officer Osgood Dahmnit (known locally as O'Dahm) was stationed at his citation writing post across the street from what passed as Fairview's town square. He stood there, as always, waiting patiently for meters to expire so he could pursue his already out-of-control Guinness world record for issuing the most parking tickets ever written by a single meter monitor in an eight-hour period. Today, Cogan would be challenging O'Dahm's territory by sliding his flyers under the same wiper blades.

O'Dahm skeptically plucked a notice from one of the cars he had just ticketed. It read:

IMPORTANT TOWN MEETING

- **If you've had it with what big corporations and special interests have done to our democracy...**

- **If you'd like to see Fairview steer a different course...**

- **Please attend a town meeting on Sunday, August 23 at 1 pm in front of the town hall to discuss what we - what you, can do about it.**

Sincerely, Sean Cogan

"What's this all about, Cogan?" quizzed O'Dahm, "Are you serious?"

Cogan sighed. It would not be the last time over the next three months he would be hearing that question.

Biting, sarcastic, unpredictable, temperamental, difficult, arrogant—these were some of the kinder terms commonly used to describe Sean Cogan. Another was hilarious. He could be very funny when he was in a good mood. He was also very smart. Twenty years before, despite an unremarkable academic career at Fairview High, but based on his ability to shout orders from the stern of a scull without falling in the water, Cogan had been admitted to Stanford University. Four years, three Pac-Ten titles, and a Head-of-the-Charles victory later, he emerged with a degree in economics.

Following graduation, he somehow got a job with the National Security Agency.

After an eight-week training program run out of a place Cogan called Bumfuc, Virginia, he was shipped off to Colombia. There he helped structure loan packages for massive projects—highways, port facilities, dams, hydroelectric plants, you name it. The programs he helped put together were characterized by the NSA as "foreign-aid projects." But before long, Cogan saw right through it. The only foreigners being aided were already living in villas—the super-elite slice of polo-playing Colombian society. After they got their cut and the local politicos peeled off another chunk, the balance went straight to handpicked American construction companies—the ones whose CEOs were constantly guffawing their way from one D.C. re-election shakedown to the next. The money eventually made its way from fancy New York banks into the offshore tax-haven accounts of mega U.S. engineering and consulting firms.

Whenever Columbia found itself having trouble on the repayment side, as was inevitable, Uncle Sam would renegotiate its loans using its latest round of leverage to strong-arm clear-cutting projects, further destroying the ancient rain forests and displacing the indigenous natives. As soon as Cogan realized what was going on behind the scenes, he bailed.

Pocketing a large "confidentiality bonus," and capitalizing on his NSA experience, he soon landed a stock-option-laden post with prestigious Mendelsohn Securities. Cogan and Mendelsohn, an investment banking and asset management firm with worldwide contacts and A-list clients, were a perfect fit. It would be hard to find a vocation, other than divorce lawyering, that rewarded egotistical aggression more than "money running." Cogan's new duties involved tracking economic trends, analyzing investment opportunities, and schmoozing with rich widows and future rich widows. He was good at all of that—especially the widows and future widows part. Rare was the day he didn't find himself being wined, dined, and mined by some deprived blond forty-something-year old with a dear friend in the breast enhancement business.

That was all great fun, and Cogan's career thrived for over a decade, right up to the day Mendelsohn was swallowed up by the Bank of America in a multi-billion dollar buyout. With his stock options suddenly worth millions, Cogan found himself awash in cash and in search of a new challenge. It didn't take long for word to spread in the start-up community that he was a potential deep pocket for promising new ventures. Soon the mountains were coming to Sir Hillary. Software companies, subdivision projects, franchise deals—the hardest part of his new career was sifting through the maze that separated genuine nuggets from fool's gold.

Having left the world of high-rise luxury space behind, Cogan returned to Fairview and purchased a pleasant brick and timber Tudor on Canyon Drive. Accessed by a wood-planked bridge, his impressive, if understated, home was bordered by a meandering creek on one side and a wildflower-blanketed hillside on the other. Gone were the Italian suits and designer shoes. Cogan's new uniform consisted of faded t-shirts, rumpled jeans, and battered sneakers. The only outward hint of success that he allowed was the high-tech, holstered cellphone that dangled from his belt like a six-gun. It rang with the bark like a St. Bernard on steroids and could provide high quality video conferencing for up to fifteen people logging on with compatible equipment from anywhere in the world.

Chris Mattington looked and acted more like a moving van driver than a newspaper reporter. A squat, burley, tough-talking New Yorker from the south side of Hell's Kitchen, he had the face of a cactus plant and the attitude of a frustrated NHL goalie waiting for the first opportunity to fly from his cage, tear across the blue line, deck somebody twice his size, and streak back to his post before the opposing team had a chance to react. In town to shop for a birthday present for his wife, Mattington found a notice on the windshield of his pockmarked Chevy and prowled around town looking for the author. He found him on the street just outside of D'Angelo's Restaurant. "You Sean Cogan?" he demanded.

"Who are you?" Cogan shot back.

"Mattington, Chris Mattington, I'm a reporter for the AP. What this?" he grunted, thrusting a crumpled copy of' Cogan's handiwork in front of him.

"It's a notice about a meeting for people who have had it with the things our government is doing."

"What things?" Mattington was scribbling on a spiral reporter's pad using a kind of shorthand that only he could decipher. Sometimes even Mattington couldn't read his own notes. What this system may have lacked in penmanship, it made up for by protecting the secrecy of Mattington's written record.

For the next hour, Mattington and Cogan stood around as the reporter fired off questions. "What's your background? Where did you go to school? Do you have a family here? Kids? Why are you doing this? What has you so upset? Why Fairview? What's the population here? How many voters are there? How do you think the locals are going to respond? If the initiative carries, then what? Are you serious about this? What type of government would run things here? What about the people who vote against the initiative?" Mattington smiled. "Will they have to move? Have you talked to any other reporters? Any broadcast media? Are you planning a press conference? Who's going to manage the campaign? What kind of organized opposition do you expect? Do you have a campaign budget?" The questions were endless.

Finally, Mattington glanced at his watch. He was done. He had a dentist's appointment. He took down Cogan's phone numbers and said he would check back in a couple of days. Thanking Cogan, Mattington shut his notepad, and climbed into his rumpled car. He wasn't going to submit anything to his editors just yet. The questions were all just for background. He was going to wait for the town meeting. Wait and see what happened. How the situation unfolded. The whole thing might well just peter out. For the moment, he just drove. Toward his dentist's office. Toward Woodridge. Toward... he smiled... toward the border.

CHAPTER THREE

MR. MAYOR

Ten at night was hardly the most convenient time of day for discussing town business. Mayor James Partida was never at his best in the late evening, and the vodka martinis he'd thrown down before arriving didn't help. But some of the participants had earlier appointments, and Partida hadn't wanted to put off discussing the Cogan situation.

Tall and skinny with a beak-like nose and flat forehead, the mayor was a walking, scowling, fidget of a man whose disorganized personality and tense demeanor were the antithesis of what one normally associates with effervescent, gladhanding politicians. His impatience with the situation at hand, coupled the strong odor of alcohol he was emitting, made everyone at the table uncomfortable.

How Partida had managed to get himself elected mayor in a place like Fairview was nothing short of bizarre. But mayor he was.

Alerted the previous day to what was happening by two unanswered messages left on his unlisted home phone from a wire services reporter seeking a comment, Partida had been caught completely by surprise. He responded by having his staff administrator throw together an urgent meeting of local business and political leaders. Most of the half-dozen people seated about the conference table knew even less about the situation than he did.

"What the hell is this all about?" he slurred to no one in particular. "Who is this Sean Cogan? Why is he doing this?" No one replied. "Who is he?" Partida repeated. "Does anyone know anything about him?"

Finally, Carl Sandgrow answered, "I know him, yes. A local guy. Big personality. Short fuse. Says corporations and the super-rich own the government. Says that we are no longer a free people, no longer a democracy. He's upset. Really upset. Says there's no way to fight back within the system. Too much money in play. Says the big guys have a stranglehold on politicians. In both parties. Seems sincere. Pretty arrogant. Very self-righteous. And what he is doing is leading a drive aimed at garnering support from all sides to have Fairview residents bail out. Vote that they have had it. That they want to steer their own course."

"Their own course? That's crazy," scowled Partida. "What's the matter with the guy? Is he nuts? This could wind up making the town look ridiculous. Like that crazy story back in the seventies about the electronic brain overhaul business down on Stanton Avenue. It took us years to live that one down. Only this time it wouldn't just be about some flighty moonchild. This time it's downright seditious." Partida paused. "What would it take to dissuade him?" The Mayor's question was typical of his approach to everything—what he meant was: *how do we just buy the guy off.*

Sandgrow got it immediately. "I don't know, Mr. Mayor," he responded. "I don't know that he's going to be dissuaded."

"What's he after? Media? Celebrity? Does he want to run for something?"

"I really doubt that he's looking for any of those things, replied Sandgro."

"Has he thought about the consequences? Does he realize..."

Carl cut him off. "I don't think he cares much about consequences, Mr. Mayor. I think he's on a mission."

"Well, mission or no mission, we've got to stop this in its goddamned tracks. This is deranged. It's sick. It's outrageous. We have to keep this nutty initiative off the ballot. It must be illegal. You can't just have people running around putting every wacky idea up for a vote. I think we should go after this guy and nail his ass. Whatever it takes." For a few long tense moments, you could hear the old pendulum down the hall ticking loudly enough to wake the mice.

"Maybe that's not the best approach," a small voice piped up from the far end of the table. "Maybe there's a smarter way to proceed."

The very idea that somebody in the room thought he was smarter than Partida was borderline seditious in itself. Paul Katz, a staunch, pro-business, card-carrying Democrat, was the founder and president of the Roundtable, a forum that hosted a highly select group of guest speakers who ran the gamut from former cabinet officers to retired network news anchors. Katz's opinions always received careful consideration.

"What if this initiative were actually to move forward?" he continued. "What if a highly publicized yea or nay vote were to be taken in a quintessentially freethinking community? And what if that vote ending up endorsing our system—as it is—by an overwhelming margin? That vote would have the exact opposite impact of what Cogan is hoping to achieve. It would be a vote of confidence in our country. A vote of confidence in America."

"But people," Partida objected, "including people in Fairview, hate big money in politics. They hate what's going on in Washington. They hate big business."

"Maybe so," replied Katz. "But these are also the same folks who stand up in the seventh inning at baseball games and belt out God Bless America like Nebraska farmers. Getting folks to vote against unpopular incumbents is one thing—getting them to vote against their country is something else. The best outcome we could ever hope for would be a staggering blow to the divisive un-American bullshit we keep hearing about. We are a country united, not divided. And this guy may be handing us a great chance to prove just that."

"But what if you're wrong?" Partida squinted. "What if the vote goes against us? I can't even start going down the parade of horrors that would result."

"I'm not wrong," Katz snapped with a condescending expression crossing his face. "I'm right. The worst thing we could do is to get heavy handed in trying to shut the guy up. That would turn him into a martyr."

The group sat, silent, trying to digest all. Finally, Wilma Nolan spoke up. A member of the town council who looked and sounded like Grannie McCoy, Nolan owned Prescott Properties, one of the largest real estate firms in the area. "Why not pursue a two-pronged approach," she said, deftly maneuvering her trademark toothpick from the left side of her mouth to the right. "Why don't we try to shut the thing down—as gently as we can—while preparing to crush it if it ever does come to a vote?"

Three or four participants quickly voiced agreement. Partida should work with a handful of carefully screened volunteers to come up with a plan to deep-six the whole thing. Katz would put together a team to work on a campaign against the ballot measure. Just in case. It was unanimous. That would be the plan. Partida didn't say anything. Maybe it was just the martinis, but it seemed to him that there was something odd about Katz's go-easy approach.

This was not a go-easy matter, thought Partida. It was not some kind of campaign to defeat a road repair bond. There was a hell of a lot more at stake here than that. This cockamamie initiative was totally unpatriotic. A challenge to our homeland!!

Cogan was nothing but a goddamned traitor. Martyr, my ass, thought Partida. People—all kinds of people—would have strong feelings about this. Not everybody was a damn wimp, like Katz. Cogan would be lucky to survive his stupid-ass initiative without getting his throat slit.

Geoffrey and Ollie were sitting in Cogan's living room as he rattled around the kitchen looking for a cheese platter. There was more to placing an initiative on the ballot than they had anticipated, but at least the rules were fairly straightforward. Quick trips to the local library and town hall had provided them with the information they needed—the requirements and procedures for qualifying local propositions for the Fairview ballot.

Geoffrey explained how the process worked. "Following submission of the draft of the initiative—which has been done—the town attorney has ten days to return to us a document called an 'Impartial Ballot Title and Summary.' At that point, we have to publish a notice of the title and summary in the local paper. After that, we can begin gathering signatures. Ten percent of the town's registered voters have to sign in order to place the initiative on the ballot for the next regularly scheduled election.

We can start the petition drive at the town meeting on August 23. Once the town clerk certifies that we have the necessary signatures, the initiative will have formally qualified for the ballot and will then appear at the time of the next regularly scheduled election on November 10."

Geoffrey said that of the 13,600 people in town, 9,371 were registered voters—4,451 Democrats, 2,574 Republicans, and 2,346 American Independent, Green Party, or Declined to State. To certify the number of signatures required, proponents usually had to garner about five percent more names than the percentages actually required. So to cover any bogus or incorrect signatures submitted, they needed to get 1,406 people to sign.

Ollie volunteered to come up with flyers for those circulating the petition to hand out. It didn't take him very long. He paraphrased words from a document that little more than two hundred years before had given inspiration to men and women of integrity and instilled fear in the hearts of tyrants . He wrote, "Governments instituted among men and women derive their just powers only from the consent of the governed. And whenever any government becomes destructive of the ends of freedom, the people have the right and duty to alter or abolish it."

"They had it right", Ollie thought. If anything, the principles they articulated were even more applicable in the world today than they had been over two hundred years before. That document, along with the ideals of those who had signed it, had been torn apart by the SOBs who had come to run things. Geoffrey and Ollie understood the process. In a little over two weeks, they would be ready to start circulating the petitions. The campaign would then be fully underway.

CHAPTER FOUR

THE PLOT

The morning after their organizational meeting at the Depot, Sean picked up his phone and autodialed. It rang six or seven times at the other end. Slowly. It was probably too early to be calling Jen at home. Maybe she was in the shower. Or still in bed. Or with some guy. Or maybe she wasn't home at all. Cogan was just about to hang up when she answered.

"Hello."

"Hi," Cogan struggled, his mind rat racing, "you, uh, sound out of breath."

Jen recognized his voice immediately. "I was just working out."

"Oh," Cogan replied, relieved she hadn't simply been having some kind of Kundalini sex with a monk half his age. "What do you do to exercise?"

"A little of this, a little of that. Aerobics, yoga, stretching, some weights. How about you?"

"Nothing. Absolutely nothing."

"You're in pretty good shape," Jen said, "for somebody who does nothing." As soon as she said it she wished she hadn't. "I mean..."

As glad as he was to hear it, Cogan let her off the hook. "I was thinking we should probably get together without all the others to talk about the legal part of this."

"Yeah, that's a good idea. The law part is probably not the most interesting aspect to most other people."

"Want to meet at your place? I could just come over whenever it's convenient"

It had been a long time since high school, a long time since Cogan had ignored her repeated advances, but there was no way Jen was going get burned again.

"Ah... Why don't we just grab a bite at Luigi's?" she suggested. "In Westborough. Do you know the place?"

"I've never eaten there but I've seen it. That's fine. We can grab some pizza or something and go through your research."

"Okay. When?"

"Seven tomorrow night? I'll pick you up?"

That sounded too much like a date to her. "Why don't I just meet you there?"

"Fine," replied Cogan, unsuccessfully trying to avoid sounding hurt. "See you there."

Cogan turned his attention to his keyboard. And his email. Junk mail drove him crazy. He received what seemed like half a dozen trash bags worth per day. None of the spam filters he was paying all that money for seemed capable of screening them out. Mortgage refinancing solicitations, stock alerts, weight-loss pills, study at-home courses, Macy's storewide sales, foreclosure listings plus the latest get rich-quick "business proposition" from a fleeing, gold-bullion-infested, son of some tiny principality's just-ousted finance minister.

Honest to God. Delete. Delete. Delete. Cogan's fingers flew across his keyboard in a blur of frenzied purpose when his IM box suddenly appeared. It was from somebody with the nickname "Moe-zus." Cogan clicked him on.

'Hi Cogan," Moe-zus began, "I got your flyer. What the hell do you think you're doing? Trying to make the U S of A look bad? If you don't like it here why don't you just get your dumb ass out? Move over to some gutless country where all the cowards can keep each other company.

"And by the way, if you have any care for survival you'll get off this dumb kick of yours before it's too late.

"Faithfully yours, Moe-zus."

As strange and grammatically challenged as the message was, it was stranger still that the sender had been able to get Cogan's personal IM address, *E-Nuffff.* It was not something he advertised on business cards. How had he gotten it? Other than spammers, only a handful of relatives and close friends knew it.

Cogan detested religious fanatics and their wacky ideas. "Hi Moe-zus," he messaged back, "want to enter my Intelligent Design Arc Building Contest? First Prize: All the McBurgers you can eat in thirty minutes.

"Hi to Noah. And by the way, it's 'you're', not 'your' and 'too', not 'to'. "Cheers, Sean"

If he had thought about it a bit more beforehand, Cogan might never have hit *Send.* Anyone calling himself "Moe-zus" and who would write such an email should probably just be left alone. Too late.

Just then Cogan's phone started barking. "Hello."

"Sean Cogan?" said a deep voice.

"Yes."

"Are you the guy involved with these flyers being passed around about a town meeting on August 23rd?"

"Yes."

"Did you do some work for the government a few years ago? In Columbia?"

Cogan stumbled. Nobody was supposed to know anything about that. That was what the confidentiality agreement had been all about. He was required to keep the whole subject of Colombia dead secret from everybody. No exceptions.

"W... where?" Cogan stuttered, sidestepping the question. But by responding as he did, he'd answered it.

"We met in Bogota," said the voice. "You didn't know it, but I was with the CIA. I'm working in the States now. I happened to be in Fairview having lunch with a friend. He told me about what you were doing. Your name sounded familiar. So I called to see if it was you. I'd like to get together."

"About what?"

"About a number of things. I don't want to talk about it on the phone."

"What's your name?" Cogan asked guardedly.

"Giller, Joseph Giller."

The name sounded familiar.

"There's something I think you should know about."

"What's that?"

"Not on the phone." Giller repeated. "Can we get together?"

"When?"

"Right now, if you'd like."

"Want to meet for coffee?"

"No, no, not with people around," Giller hesitated. Cogan was taken aback by the alarm in his voice. "We can just go for a walk. Let's meet at Boyle Park. I have to run a fast errand first. Can you be there around one?"

"I'll see you then. In front of the park, by the tennis courts."

"I'll be in a gray Ford Explorer" said Giller. "Nondescript except for the pirate flag on the antenna." Pirate flag??

"OK," Cogan began... "But could you..." The line went dead just as another chat message from Moe-zus popped open. *Crap.*

"What do you have against God?" Moe-zus railed.

"I don't have anything against God," Cogan typed back. "I just can't stand organized religions."

"Why?"

"They brainwash people, argue about things no one can prove, use scare tactics to coerce members into blind obedience, divide people into opposing camps, engage in absurd rituals, encourage overpopulation, justify maintaining the status quo, discriminate against women, use tax exemptions to fund partisan political agendas, preach hatred, perpetuate ignorance, and put ridiculous hats on their leaders. Plus, of course, they justify killing people in the name of God. Other than that, I guess they're okay."

What could Moe-zus say in the face of such an articulate and measured response? "Screw you."

Cogan was not in the mood for serious conversation with a bible-thumper. "That's not very nice," he taunted. "What would St. Francis say?"

"What's wrong with St. Francis?"

"Nothing, I guess. Doesn't everybody carry on conversations with birdies?"

If it was possible to splutter on a keyboard, Moe-zus was doing it. "You're sick. You're damned sick!!!" he typed.

"Right," replied Cogan. "I'm sick. And loonies screaming, jumping, and falling to the floor in a frenzy are normal. Exorcisms are normal. Suicide bombers are normal. Burning witches is normal. Celibacy is normal. The Crusades were normal. Speaking in tongues is normal. All of that is normal. Right?"

Moe-zus avoided answering. "Religion is a good thing," he typed. "It teaches people honesty, integrity, fairness. It teaches that there is more to life than acquiring money and power. It teaches people to treat each other decently. It teaches people to help the poor. To clothe the needy. To feed the hungry."

"Camel dung," typed Cogan. Moe-zus was still typing.

"You are a sick, sick person, Cogan," he replied. "Religion is a good thing for people. And religious people are a good thing for America. You are wrong to attack religion. And you are wrong to attack America. God will punish you. You'll see. You just wait. You just wait."

ENOUGH, Cogan thought as he hit the off switch. Goddamned kook.

Boyle Park was Fairview's Jock Central. Four or five years earlier, a local rock star with a kid in the Little League had decided that the park's baseball field, with its divots, bumps, rocks, weeds, and dilapidated stands, was in dire need of renovation. A few weeks and a single overflow concert later, the money had been raised. Very quickly, a newly manicured playing field framed by real dugouts, old fashioned bleachers, a huge outfield scoreboard, and a state-of-the-art refreshment stand had been completed.

To the south of the baseball field, close to Central Avenue and adjacent to a children's playground featuring slides, monkey bars, swings, and more, there were half a dozen inviting tennis courts. Cogan arrived at 12:54. He sat waiting in his car, scanning the morning paper.

At precisely one, a gray Explorer rolled up, pirate flag flapping in the breeze. A short stocky man in his 50s, who looked like a combination of Sylvester Stallone and Danny DeVito, emerged. Strong and serious-looking, he reminded Cogan of a rugby player—complete with the requisite scars on his forehead. The scars, however, were not from rugby. Cogan extended his hand, and the man shook it like a steelworker.

"Joseph Giller," he announced. "Thanks for meeting me on such short notice."

"It sounded important," replied Cogan.

"It is," replied Giller, glancing around furtively. "There's a lot going on, and I don't know what you know and don't know, or why you're doing what you're doing. So I wanted to find out. What is your flyer was about? Tell me about it."

"It's pretty simple. I've just had it with big money running the country. I think it's very scary."

"How do you mean?" quizzed Giller. "What are you specifically referring to?"

"You know, crooked politicians, greedy CEOs, laws written by lobbyists... all the things we read about. I've just finally had it. This is not the country I grew up in. The whole system is corrupt. I can't stand it anymore."

Giller looked disappointed. "Anything else?" he asked, eyebrows rising as he cleared his throat, "besides what you've read in the papers?"

"Well..." Cogan paused, "I'm also very upset with the government's use of voicemail."

"Voicemail?" said Giller, a touch of incredulity in his voice. "You're upset with the government because of voicemail?"

"You can't get a normal human on the phone anymore. No matter who you're trying to call or what department, you get voicemail. Some long-winded irrelevant tape recording. The IRS is a perfect example. 'Your call is important to us,' they lie. Then they say: 'If you are calling about a change of address, press one; if you are calling about obtaining an extension, press two; if you are calling about an overdue refund, press three; if your call is about a pending audit, press four; if you have questions concerning deductions, press five,' and on and on and on. Then they finally tell you to hit twenty if you want to speak to a customer service representative—*customer service*! At the IRS? Talk about a self-cancelling phrase. Then an infant comes on the line. Some twenty-year old with such a heavy accent that you can't even understand her. And she knows absolutely nothing and is clearly reading from a script. And before you can say a word, she puts you on hold. Then you are forced to listen to Muzak. To Leslie Gore or Tom Jones or somebody ancient, and it's pure torture. And you can't hang up so you are forced to listen. And that goes on for fifteen minutes. Then you're cut off. Cut off! Suddenly you're talking to a dial tone. So you have to hang up and start all over again. It's the same thing with every damned agency and department in the whole damn government."

Giller couldn't believe his ears. "And you want to pass this initiative because of that? And because of voicemail?"

"No, no," protested Cogan, a tad embarrassed, "it's just one of the things I'm upset about. But I'm not planning on pressing that as a major issue in the campaign. The other things are... are... more important."

"Right," Giller responded. "What about form letters? Are you upset about form letters too?"

"No," Cogan shot back, sensing a trap. "Form letters are okay."

Giller seemed taken aback by all of this. It wasn't what he had expected. But he wasn't easily deterred. Besides, he had his own agenda. With his CIA background, Giller saw the world as a four-dimensional chess match, not a game of checkers. He needed more information about just how bright Cogan was and whether he'd be able to handle what was coming.

"Other than in Bogota," he said, "have you ever worked for the government?"

"No, why?"

"I've been with the CIA for fourteen years. At Langley and all over."

"Doing what?"

"I can't talk about specifics. But generally, information gathering. Sometimes on behalf of the U.S., sometimes on behalf of foreign governments."

"Where?"

"South and Central America. The Arab world. Iraq, Iran, Saudi Arabia."

"What do you mean by 'information gathering'? What kinds of information?"

"Political, economic, personal, religious, demographic, all of it. Obtaining data— all kinds of data—for elaborate computerized crystal balls used to project and predict things."

"Other than for projections, what did you do with the information?"

"M and I. Manipulation and Intimidation. Extortion. Bribery. That sort of thing."

"I've heard," bluffed Cogan, "about some private sector outfit that does stuff that's too hot even for the CIA."

"Sometimes," confirmed Giller, "on especially sensitive projects, we work with a private organization, a private company, run by a guy—by a highly connected D.C. big hat. It gets involved in projects so controversial there's a need to avoid all oversight. Because it's private, it reports to no one."

"Why are you telling me this?"

"Because I've grown very concerned. I recently learned that the government maintains detailed personal files—not just on people suspected of criminal activities—but on all kinds of people. Even its own," Giller paused, "its own intelligence agents for example. People like me.

"I was anonymously sent a copy of my file. And I couldn't believe it. Bank records, prescription drug records, video surveillance, a political profile, lists of books purchased, transcripts of conversations in my car recorded from the speaker system for my cellphone, wiretaps of conversations with my ex, with my kids, with friends, with my family therapist, with accountants, attorneys, doctors..."

"Conversations you had in your car?"

"Yeah. They know everything that goes on in your car. They can even take satellite control of it through the computer systems installed by the manufacturer."

"But why? Why would the government do that?

"One can only guess. But in some countries we used to do it to build dossiers on people—so that if it ever became necessary, the government would know just who to round up. So it could put people where they couldn't cause problems, or so they could just disappear. It was one thing for us to be doing some of these things overseas. But here? Now?"

"But... who..."

"FBI. NSA. Homeland Security. This CenTel operation..."

"CenTel...?"

Giller pretended it was just a slip of the tongue. Cogan correctly assumed it was intentional.

"In any case, point is things are really fucked up. Totally out of whack," Giller said.

"Aren't you concerned that—that they might be recording you right now?"

"They picked on the wrong guy," Giller replied. "The wrong guy for this assignment. I don't think they know I'm aware of my file. And I know how to incapacitate their surveillance equipment so that they'll think it just blew a battery.

"But they can still follow you. They would know you're meeting here with me."

"They're probably watching right now," Giller conceded, "but they won't think that's odd."

"Why not?"

"Figure it out."

"What?"

"Suffice it to say that I didn't just happen to wander into Fairview to have lunch."

Cogan paused, confused. Then it suddenly hit him. "You were sent here? By the people you work for?"

"I didn't say that," Giller replied, staring straight ahead.

Cogan felt like he'd been hit in the chest. "To spy? On me?" He was incredulous. "This is insane."

"I'm not acknowledging any such thing," replied Giller. "But like I said, things are out of whack. Some folks in high places are really paranoid—about all kinds of things. All kinds of people. Writers, entertainers, activists, even some mainstream politicians. You wouldn't believe the extent of it. You need to be careful. I'm not exaggerating. Watch your back.

"Listen to me. You're going to be getting a package. A plain package— no postage. No return address. Printed instructions. It will arrive at your house. Don't blow it off. Don't ignore it. Just follow the instructions. I've gotta go."

Suddenly, without warning, Giller started to leave.

"Wait. How can I contact you?"

Giller said nothing. He turned on his heel, strode back to his car, got in, and drove off. As he headed down the street, pirate flag once again flapping in the wind, Cogan stood there in shock. He noticed for the first time the dryness in his mouth and the slight trembling in his hands. He also noticed a beat up Chevy Suburban parked half a block away. It was just sitting there by the side of the road in a red public-transit no-parking zone. Too bad O'Dahm wasn't around. A bus zone tag was a two-hundred-dollar ticket. It would have made his day.

Mark Fischer, a clean, wiry, freckle-faced, redhead, was raised by devout parents in a ranch-style house in a 1950s subdivision just inside Fairview's town limits. Mark's mother was a stay-at-home mom and his father, a retired Air Force lifer, was working for Allied over in Richardson. Thoughtful and straight shooting, Fischer had always been a smart kid. Straight As. Smart but somehow odd. Excessively clean cut with perfect posture and diction, he was the kind of guy that would say "Yes, I shall be going to the game," rather than "Yeah, I'll be there."

Before he graduated from high school, Fischer had rarely set foot beyond a hundred miles of his home. But when several Ivy League schools suddenly started throwing unexpected solicitations his way, he decided to have a look around. He fell for New England instantly. He loved it. After checking out half a dozen universities from Maine to Connecticut, he finally settled on Brown. With its pristine setting in Providence, architectural beauty, and healthy endowment, Brown had lured professors of international renown to Rhode Island. Their encouragement over four years inspired Mark to teach, and his religious background led him to do so with a Catholic Mission. He wound up in a small African village just south of Nairobi. At the moment, he was on summer break, back home for a short visit to reconnect with old friends and attend a big party for his parents' thirty-fifth wedding anniversary.

Driving around Fairview, with its trendy boutiques and Italian bistros, was like an out-of-body experience for him. Two days earlier, he had been standing by a bonfire, listening to lion grunts and struggling to keep rhythm with grinning tribal drummers. A far cry from designer jeans and mocha javas.

As he turned the corner at Williams and Prospect, his path was suddenly blocked by a small anti-war demonstration. A few dozen people were carrying signs protesting U.S. Middle East policy. One huge banner proclaimed "No More Blood for Oil." Another read "Enough war profiteering" Demonstrators were waiving at cars, franticly pumping their signs up and down. Mark was stunned: What's the matter with these people? Why don't they understand? What do they want us to do? Just roll over? Give up? Let the crazies win?

He pulled off to the side of the road and got out of the car. Approaching one of the leaders, he took a deep breath. "Look," he said stiffly, "you have every right to express your opinions, but so do I. And I think you are naïve beyond words. Have you ever talked to one of these Muslim extremists? Do you have any idea how outside of our world they are? Do you understand their agenda? Do you realize that they want to destroy everything you believe in? Do you realize that they want to crush every semblance of life as you know it? We are fighting one of the most sinister forces in the history of civilization. These are people who randomly murder their own. Randomly. They blow up children in markets, schools, even mosques. They pry off the fingernails of prisoners, innocent people that they kidnap. Civilians. They saw off people's heads. They tie their legs apart and set their testicles on fire. They burn their flesh with flaming branding irons. They make them watch as their children are killed and their wives are gang-raped."

A small crowd started to gather, sensing trouble.

"I'm sorry if I'm disturbing your little demonstration. And like I said, it's your right to be parading around with whatever kind of signs you want. But I'll tell you something. I've just traveled here from halfway around the world. I know what these people are like." Fischer was on a roll. The fact that he had never been anywhere other than New York, Rhode Island, and Kenya didn't slow him down. "Go to Afghanistan," he ranted, "to Somalia, Iraq, Saudi Arabia... try waving protest signs around there. And see what happens."

The demonstrator, whoever he was, a young man with a sweet, innocent face and easy manner, said nothing. He just stood there with an almost blank expression. Several of his fellow demonstrators reacted the same way. Just then, a young woman walked up and started communicating with them in sign language.

"Shit." Fisher muttered, "They're deaf." Deaf demonstrators. They hadn't heard a word. Shaking his head in frustration, he trudged back to his car and took off.

CHAPTER FIVE

LUIGI'S

Luigi's was as Italian a restaurant as you could ever find. With a tiny reception and waiting area and small wooden tables spaced practically on top of each other, framed by six booths and a large serving table, it resonated with the background voice of Placido Domingo and reeked of fresh garlic and spices. The owner, Emilio, was the cook, waiter, and sometimes the dishwasher. Cogan arrived first. Ten minutes later Jen stormed in like an Italian movie star, planting a kiss on Emilio's cheek.

"Emilio," she teased, waving her arms and gesturing as she slid into Cogan's booth, "what are you waiting for? A bottle of my favorite Chianti."

Emilio dished it right back.

"Hey, you disappear for so long we all figure you died, and then you just fly in here from nowhere and expect me to remember your favorite Chianti. Forget it. I have something better than whatever that was anyway," he grinned. Scanning the long wine rack displaying dozens of bottles, Emilio quickly found what he was looking for. Ignoring Cogan, he poured a taste for Jen and stood back proudly.

"It's a Barolo. The king of wines. From the hills outside of Piedmont, north of Tuscany. Tell me what you think?"

Jen swirled it around in her glass, breathed in the wine's distinctive aroma, and took a slow sip, waiting for a moment to allow the taste to linger. "Nice," she said, "very nice."

"It's good," agreed Emilio as he filled her glass.

"So who is this?" he asked, nodding toward Cogan and sizing him up with a skeptical eye. "A new boyfriend?"

"No way," replied Jen. "I learned my lesson with this one back in high school. He's just a business acquaintance."

"Uh-huh," Emilio laughed.

"Well," attempted Cogan, "I don't recall…"

"Let's order," interrupted Jen, "I recommend the capellini ala Gino or the linguini primavera."

"OK," Cogan said, "I'll have the capellini."

"And I'll have the linguini," Jen said.

"Excellent." Emilio filled Cogan's glass without asking and disappeared into the kitchen.

"What lesson in high school?" Cogan feigned.

"You know very well what lesson."

Cogan studied the tablecloth while Jen let him squirm.

"Okay. To evaluate the approach we are taking with the initiative I started by examining the history of federalism and the issue of states rights.

For fifteen minutes she talked nonstop. About disagreements among the Framers of the Constitution over the role of government, and how most of them were wary of ceding power to a centralized authority.

"Because of their experience with the Crown?" said Cogan.

"Right. There were big arguments about what powers should be delegated to the federal government versus those that should be retained by the states—and by the people themselves." Jen read short excerpts from the writings of Alexander Hamilton, John Jay, and James Madison. "They were concerned about the federal government growing too powerful. About exactly the kind of thing that is going on now," she said.

"And that has been going on for a long, long time."

Jen had done her homework. The woman was brilliant. Brilliant and beautiful. Brilliant, beautiful and as distant as the Great Barrier Reef.

"Over the years there have been a number of ways that local political entities have sought independence from larger authorities. Rarely have efforts gone beyond the early stages, but they have included proposals to divide California into two, three, and even four states.

"In 1849, part of Kentucky asked its legislature to permit it to join Virginia. Eastern Massachusetts has repeatedly attempted to split from Western Massachusetts.

Residents of the Nebraska panhandle have threatened to leave Nebraska and join Wyoming. And parts of Colorado, Georgia, Illinois, Kansas, New York, New Jersey,

New Hampshire, Connecticut, Tennessee, Texas, Utah, Vermont, Virginia, Washington, and Wisconsin have all proposed sectioning off and either joining neighboring states or forming their own state."

Cogan sat there shocked that the notion that independence movements had such a colorful history. He had no idea. "Sounds like this idea has been around for a while," he said.

"Yes," Jen said, taking another sip, "and no."

Emilio appeared with their steaming entrées. "Buon appetito," he said.

"Grazie," Jen nodded, smiling broadly. But she wasn't about to slow down. "Virtually all of these examples have involved either quitting a state and joining another or forming a new one. Almost all have also involved taxation, representation, gerrymandering, or boundary disputes. But forming a new tiny state, even if you could do it, wouldn't solve the problem. The new state would still be subject to the higher authority of the federal government – to laws enacted by Congress and to the rulings of federal courts including the U S Supreme Court..."

"Like court decisions ruling that U S politicians have the constitutional right to accept payoffs from foreign drug lords or saying that corporations have the same constitutional rights as people?"

"Right. So even if we could do it, whether we form a new 'state' or not, we would still be subject to the same federal laws and court decisions that we have to live with now. So that wouldn't accomplish anything."

"I get it."

"Another option would be to attempt to withdraw from the Union entirely. In terms of states or portions of states forming separate autonomous entities, there have actually been minor movements of one kind or another to do that in parts of the Pacific Northwest, California, Alaska, Hawaii, portions of the Southwest, and of course in Vermont. But from what I've seen so far, the only real effort in the U.S. to do that was the one that led to the Civil War. So that is not an option, either.

"A third possibility would be a kind of end run. Fairview's actual borders were set by the State Constitution. It reads like a plot map: '... commencing at the intersection of the 42nd degree of north latitude with the 120th degree of longitude west and running south...' blah, blah, blah. We could just propose an amendment to the current state constitution that would revise the borders to exclude Fairview and rearrange the State's perimeter to carve us right out."

"So Fairview would no longer be a part of our state, but would be a kind of the proverbial no mans' land?"

"Something like that..."

"That would seem like kind of a chicken-shit approach to me. And not very doable. We're a lot more likely to win a local vote than a statewide one."

Emilio approached their table. "Everything OK?"

"Delicioso," Jen said.

"Wonderful," added Cogan.

"So that brings us back to the idea of civil disobedience. Like with the civil rights movement. But on an official scale. Where the town of Fairview, as a government entity, simply refuses to go along with laws and court decisions that by a vote of our residents, we deem to be totally unacceptable. So that is where I came out in my research. The approach we are taking with the initiative as it's worded is the best approach.

"Okay. Good. Works for me."

Cogan topped off both glasses as the Brunello's hearty aroma filtered into the air.

"I'll toast to that," he grinned. "Great work. Thank you."

"Now let me tell you what happened after we spoke this morning."

"What?"

Cogan proceeded to report the story about Joseph Giller. The phone call, the meeting, the Ford Explorer, the pirate flag, the conversation. Jen just looked at him, stunned.

"What do you think about it?" she asked. "Do you believe it?"

"If it isn't true, the guy is a hell of a liar. And if it is true, the country is even worse off than I imagined."

"How do you want to deal with the town meeting?" she asked.

"I guess we have to just play it by ear. God only knows what kind of response we're going to get. Bring a flak jacket just in case."

"You know," Jen replied, "it's not too late to punt. We can rewrite the initiative into a political-reform referendum specifically targeting lobbying, environmental policies, campaign finance, election oversight, that kind of thing."

"No way," laughed Cogan, "that would be like Paul Revere whispering: 'The British are coming; the British are coming' over his backyard fence."

"Okay," Jen laughed. "Anyway, I hope this was helpful. I'll keep working on it. Let me know what you want me to focus on."

"Okay." Jen was looking at her watch. "How about some dessert?" Cogan asked.

"Maybe next time. I've gotta go."

"But..."

"I'm sorry. I didn't realize how late it was. I have to get up early in the morning."

"But..."

Before he could respond, Jen dropped a wad of bills on the table and headed toward the door. "That should cover my half," she smiled. "See you soon, Sean. Ciao," she called back to Emilio.

"Ciao," Emilio called after her.

When the door closed Emilio cast a warm smile at Cogan. "She likes you, eh?"

"I don't think so," Cogan replied.

"I do," Emilio said. "And I'm Italian. I know women."

Sitting at his kitchen table, Cogan listened to his voice mail. There was a long message from Danielle describing what she, Geoffrey, and Ollie had learned about initiative and proposition requirements and reporting on their petition plans.

Cogan picked up his phone. When he told Danielle about his encounter with Mattington, the AP reporter, her reaction was strong.

"I know Mattington," she said. "He's no local hack. His stuff goes out to hundreds of media outlets nationwide. Articles under his byline are scrutinized by a lot of people. Reporters like him are really information filters," she cautioned. "If Mattington likes you, he can make you out to be sincere, dedicated, and forthright. If he doesn't, he can portray you as a nutty whacko. Two things are important here. Message and demeanor. Whenever you talk to him—or any reporter—it's important to control the message, stay on point, and avoid being distracted or baited. You have to have your talking points down cold. You need to come off as reasonable, thoughtful, rational, even self-deprecating. Assume you're going to be attacked with aggressive, sarcastic questions. You have to stand up to it, unblinking. Avoid at all costs coming across as a zealot, an extremist, a radical.

"Remember that what we are proposing here is not crazy. All we want is a government that represents us instead of big money. A government of integrity, not of lies. A government of honor, not of corruption. A government we can believe in and not fear. That's all the Founders wanted. We are the patriots. We are the ones who are right. Stick to those themes, and you'll be fine."

CHAPTER SIX

NO OLIVER WENDELL HOLMES

William Creswell was no Oliver Wendell Holmes. A journeyman lawyer with a JD from some anonymous law school that was barely a cut above the places that advertise on matchbook covers. He had landed a job in the town attorney's office on the strength of his megabuck developer father's political muscle. Twelve years later, his first boss having died and that boss's replacement having quit to open a gas station, Creswell found himself heading up the office. Running the place with a part-time assistant who hadn't yet finished his first year of law school, Creswell's principal duty as town attorney consisted of attending town council meetings to answer questions about permit applications. The only courtroom he'd ever seen on the inside was the one where he had been sworn in as a lawyer following his sixth swing at the bar exam. Rumor had it that he would still be swinging if his old man hadn't hired the head of the Committee of Bar Examiners as his company's general counsel. Of the over 179,000 card-carrying attorneys in the state, it was doubtful that any of them would have wanted to replace him. To call his job a dead-end street was like calling the county dump a trashcan. But as boring as his work was, Creswell took solace in the job security.

Whenever the phone rang—a rare occurrence—Creswell answered it himself. Usually it was a telemarketer or the wrong number. So he was shocked to pick it up and hear the voice of Mayor Partida on the line. When Partida announced that he needed help on a special project, Creswell dropped the phone.

"Yes, Sir, Y-Your Honor," he stuttered when he'd picked it up. "What can I do?"

Partida explained the Cogan situation and its possible ramifications. If this whole thing wasn't nipped in the bud, he said, it could spin right out of control. It was just the kind of thing the media might try to turn into a six-ring circus. Partida wanted to enlist Creswell to, as he put it, "solve the problem."

"Got it. Got it," assured Creswell. "I'll handle it. It's, uhh, it's under control."

"Great," Partida replied. "I knew you could take care of this. I knew I could depend on you."

"I know just what to do." Creswell assured the mayor. But he knew no such thing. And when he replaced the receiver, he found himself sitting alone in his office, confused. He didn't know where to start. The hallway door clicked open, and Creswell suddenly remembered. Thank God it was Monday. His assistant didn't have any morning classes on Mondays. Jeb Holngrin could figure this out.

"Mornin', Bill" said Jeb, his bloodshot eyes and scratchy-looking beard indicating that he'd had a late night.

"No time for that," Creswell replied. "We've got a problem."

"Toilet stopped up again?"

"No, I mean a real problem, Jeb." Creswell laid it all out while Jeb nodded his head up and down, pretending to understand. The two of them just sat there. Thinking.

"I've got it," Jeb offered. "Let's look at the statute."

"What statute?"

"Under the municipal code. The initiative statute. I'll be right back."

Jeb withdrew to his cubicle to download Sean Cogan's initiative file and to bang away on Lexus-Nexus, the modern equivalent of a law library.

He emerged twenty minutes later with a printout. "We don't have to do anything at all for several days," Jeb announced. "The initiative was filed on August 10, and we have a total of ten days to write what's called the initiative's 'Title and Summary.' Until we write that, the proponents of the initiative won't have anything they can publish in the newspaper. And until it's published in the paper, they can't start collecting signatures. Look," he said, "it's all spelled out right here in the statute."

"So how does that help us?"

"What if we just don't give them their title and summary? There'd be nothing for them to publish, and so they couldn't start gathering signatures. What if we simply refuse to approve the initiative? We can say that it's unconstitutional, and thus we won't put it on the ballot. Then they'll have to sue us. And even if we lose, we can appeal. It will take months, maybe years. Election Day will be a distant memory. We'd be able to find other ways to deep-six this, too. Invalid signatures, problems with notices, problems with time requirements. Whatever. We can run these guys around in circles until they collapse."

"Brilliant," gushed Creswell. "Just brilliant." Creswell was ecstatic. He was going to be a hero. What he had promised Mayor Partida was actually going to turn out to be true. Partida would be thrilled. But first, Creswell needed to figure out what he wanted from the deal. Maybe he should ask for a raise. Or better yet, a fat bonus. He wouldn't mention it right away. It would be better to let things unfold for a bit.

So, he and the mayor could just savor it.

Most members of the town council thought of him as a lightweight. "Restwell," they called him behind his back. As though he had just sauntered in from the cornfields. Ha! He was smarter than people thought. A lot smarter. And this was his chance to demonstrate that for all to see. "Mr. Mayor?" he practiced, clearing his throat. "Creswell, here. I've solved your problem, Sir. Wait until you hear..."

He'd work on it a bit more, polishing his delivery. Then he'd call Partida. Boy, would the mayor be thrilled.

CHAPTER SEVEN

SHIATSU

Cogan didn't even try to play it cool. At six sharp, the night after their get together at Luigi's, he was on the phone again. Again, she was out of breath. "Exercising?" he laughed.

"Maybe," Jen laughed. "What's up?"

Following an uncomfortable silence, he said it. "Look, I think you need to let go."

"Of what?"

"Of being pissed off at me about high school."

"I don't know what you're talking about," Jen lied.

"Yes, you do. And you're punishing me because of it. And I'm a good guy. And I don't deserve it."

"What..."

"I'm coming over. Right now. And we're going to have it out and get this over with." He laughed. "What's your address?"

Jen was shocked.

"C'mon," Cogan repeated, "give me your address?"

Before she could think, she'd said "All right, but it's not going to do you any good."

"We'll see. What is it?"

"340 Chestnut. White house with gray trim. There's a three-foot

Buddha by the front door. "But Sean..."

Click.

Buddha was right there by the front door. Round and grinning, hands raised to the heavens. More like four-feet tall than three. Jen opened the door wearing a battered sweatshirt and baggy jeans. Her glasses sat low on her nose, and her long auburn hair went every direction at once. She was clutching more notes and a legal pad. She looked great. "I picked up a bottle of that Barolo," Cogan said, grinning.

Jen's living room was filled with art and mementos from trips around the world. On one wall was a poster-size blowup of a photo that looked like it was taken in the Himalayas. Grinning Sherpas surrounded by packs and mountaineering gear and Jen with her arms around them, beaming.

She took out her new wine glasses. It wouldn't hurt to try them out. She motioned Cogan toward the couch and sat down opposite him on a wicker easy chair. She handed him a corkscrew. "So, what are you crawling over here to say?"

"Trawling?" Cogan asked, pretending not to understand.

"I know," Jen said, "there's something wrong with the acoustics in here. I said crawling."

At least she was no longer in denial. That was a start. He skipped the tasting part and just poured two glasses. "Here's to Fairview," he toasted, "Land of the Free..."

"... and home of the independence movement," Jen finished. As they sipped, she stared at him in self-righteous silence. Ten or fifteen long seconds passed.

"All right," he said, "I'm sorry."

"Sorry? Sorry?" deadpanned Jen. "But whatever for?"

"C'mon, Jen. Knock it off."

"Un-uh," Jen replied, taking another sip. It really was a nice wine. She couldn't believe she actually had Cogan squirming. No way was she going to let him off the hook. "How sorry?"

"Damn it. Terribly, completely, indescribably, wildly, deeply, very..."

"So what are you going to do about it?" she asked.

Cogan paused, biting his lip. "Buy you more Barolo?"

"More... Barolo?"

"With baguettes and brie and foie gras?"

How could she resist? "Triple crème?"

"OK, triple crème. Am I forgiven?"

"You just want sex," Jen replied.

That wasn't true. Exactly.

"Actually, I want to see what kind of shiatsu you can do. I have a bad back. Old basketball injury."

'Right," sniffed Jen.

"No, really. It's true"

"You could never handle one of my massages." Jen laughed.

"Want to bet?"

"No way," she said, refilling both glasses, "it's not going to be that easy."

As the first hint of morning light filtered through Jen's living-room shutters, Cogan opened his eyes with the disorientation of a waking-dead person. His back hadn't felt better in years. Slowly gathering his awareness, he silently pulled himself out from under the thin blanket that had been placed over him. He walked across the living room to Jen's bedroom. Jen was asleep, the covers pulled high over her head.

"I've got to get over to my place," he whispered. "Is that okay?"

"Mmmm."

"Call you in an hour or so?"

"Mmmm."

"You all right?"

"Mmmm."

She looked beautiful.

"Mmmm," he mocked.

As Cogan walked to his car, his mind suddenly shifted into overdrive for no apparent reason. How had he gotten himself involved in all of this? Was Giller right? Was he in over his head? What would happen when the story hit the media?

CHAPTER EIGHT

CEN TEL

Except for having no listing of its name in the building directory or anywhere else, at first glance the office suite looked pretty normal. With its assortment of desks, cubicles, computers, and telephones, it might well have been a real estate brokerage or insurance agency or any other business. Closer inspection, however, revealed something entirely different. CenTel's space, which exuded the unmistakable odor of half-eaten nachos and stale chicken wings, was jammed with electronic equipment, cable wiring, surveillance cameras, and motion detectors. An entire wall consisted of a huge flat screen capable of producing God-only-knows what kind of images and information.

A sweaty, frowning, short-sleeved caricature of some set designer's idea of a hatchet man, Alfonse Renaldo Bruno stood leaning over his huge desk. Of medium height, with a full head of dark, straight hair, and weighing in at 257, Bruno worked out daily with free weights and equipment. He looked and acted like he could bench-press a small bus. You would never guess that he was the proud owner of a huge collection of antique Beanie Babies. He had been amassing them—thousands of them—since the 1980s. His favorite, with red hair and wearing a blue and white striped t-shirt and navy shorts, was named Booper.

At the moment, Bruno was clutching a remote to the massive communications system spread out across his oversized credenza. The console itself was a work of art. Equipped with more buttons than could possibly have any function, it was programmed with the speed dials of hundreds of phone numbers all connected to coded names. Bruno was one of just three people with access to the codes.

There were no receptionists, secretaries, or staff assistants in sight. Just fifty-six, bright- eyed, thoroughly screened, security-cleared, meticulously groomed, highly paid 'deputies.'

He picked up a piece of paper and studied it. Although the author of the memo he was reading wasn't identified, Bruno knew exactly who it was. David Henninger, his boss, the director of CenTel and one of the most invisible, connected people in Washington.

What was going on in Fairview wasn't the kind of thing that happened every day. And important people wanted Bruno to get the details. The idea of an entire town contemplating a 'screw you' initiative like this was the kind of silliness that could stir up some real problems. It wasn't the only whacko movement bouncing around, but it was a very troublesome one. It had the potential to really spin out of control.

It didn't take long for Bruno to set things in motion. He directed Chino Vasquez and Chuck McMann, two experienced agents, to work up files on all the major players. "I'm especially interested," he said, "in five individuals: Sean Cogan, Jennifer Renton, Geoffrey Santorum, Danielle Hall, and Ollie Watterson. Take all precautions," he ordered. "Avoid detection. No direct contact."

Back in Fairview, Paul Katz realized that he needed some help. Someone who would be loyal, trustworthy and of unquestionable integrity. Someone who was really smart. Someone who could organize and coordinate everything. Someone who could manage and run interference. Someone who could make damn sure this stupid initiative went up in flames.

He knew exactly where to go. Paul had known the Fischer family for years. They were as solid as they came. Strong values, committed to principle, courageous, good, decent, dependable, patriotic, religious people. He knew that Mark was doing missionary work in Kenya. He had run into him just yesterday at Starbuck's for the first time in years. He was a good kid. And smart. Had flown all the way from Africa to attend his parents' anniversary celebration. He was the guy. He would be here for at least the summer. Perhaps he could be persuaded to stay on through Election Day.

At town hall, Creswell and Holngrin were busily reading and rereading the Constitution. Foraging for wording that would preclude political subdivisions from withdrawing from the Union. For a provision that would make the initiative unconstitutional. They weren't having any luck. There was no such language in the document.

CHAPTER NINE

WORRIED

Although Paul Katz wasn't on the town council, he was close to several of the members. So close that it didn't take him long to hear about what Partida and Creswell were up to. By pretending to be a supporter of their tactical plan, he had actually gotten Creswell to admit—no, to brag—about it.

Sitting in his family room, surrounded by dozens of photos taken with former heads of state, cabinet members, newscasters, sports heroes, movie stars, and others who had graced his speakers bureau over the years, Katz settled into his La-Z-Boy and prepared himself for the unpleasant conversation he was about to initiate. Partida answered on the third ring.

"Jimmy," Katz said, "how are you doing?" He tried unsuccessfully to pretend he cared about the answer.

"Fine" replied His Honor, not bothering to reciprocate.

"Jimmy, I'm worried about what Creswell is up to. In my opinion, it's exactly the kind of thing that could really bite us in the ass. If people wind up thinking that opponents of this initiative are resorting to heavy-handed or dirty tactics, they could react adversely. They could well be driven right into the enemy camp. I think it would be a big mistake. You shouldn't let him do it."

Partida was not in the mood to be lectured. And he hated being addressed as

Jimmy. His name was not Jimmy. It was James. James, or Mayor, or Mr. Mayor, or

Mayor Partida, or simply Sir. Not Jimmy. Jimmy was condescending. Especially the way Katz pronounced it. He made it sound like he was talking to some sweaty country-club car-parking attendant. He sounded so self-assured, so self-righteous, so holier-than-thou. It drove Partida crazy. Besides, Katz was a goddamned wimp. An intellectual and a wimp. But that, smiled Partida to himself, was redundant.

"I'll think about it," Partida lied.

Right, thought Katz. *You'll think about it. For about four seconds. Then you'll just plow on straight ahead. Mr. Tough Guy*. But the problem with Partida wasn't that he was tough. The problem was that he was stupid.

"I hope you will." Katz taunted. "I hope you will think about it. It wouldn't be a very smart move." That was all Katz had to say. For the second time in a week, he had implied that he was smarter than Partida. Who did he think he was?

"I've always meant to ask you," inquired Partida, a bit too snidely, "where did you go to school to give you such confidence in the wisdom of your analyzing of things?"

"Wisdom of your analyzing of things?" Katz couldn't believe his ears. Partida was truly beyond dumb.

"USC. Why?"

Partida smiled. Here was his chance. It was too bad there wasn't an audience for this. It was too bad it was just the two of them. Wait until Katz heard the words Partida was about to utter. He wished he could see the expression on Katz's face.

"I went to Cornell," Partida said. "The same year as former President Bush. W Bush. And," he added, "I was also a member of Cross and Dagger

"Quill and Dagger," corrected Katz. And he went to Yale, not Cornell.

"Whatever," responded Partida, pushing the tape recorder out of the way to make more room for his fourth vodka martini. *Cross and Dagger, Quill and Dagger,* Cornell, Yale…what difference did it make? It was a secret society anyway. That was the point.

CHAPTER TEN

BEGINNING TO UNDERSTAND

Early on Tuesday morning, August 18, Cogan drove by town hall to see if the notice of title and summary was done. Laurie Feinton, the town clerk he'd met when he dropped off the initiative, said she would find out. She disappeared into the town attorney's office and shut the door. Cogan, sitting in the waiting area and straining to hear their muffled conversation, had the uneasy feeling that something was going on behind the scenes. Something he knew nothing about.

His thoughts drifted back to his meeting with Giller. Was the guy telling the truth? Maybe he was exaggerating. Maybe he was delusional. His warnings sounded dire, but Cogan hadn't noticed anything unusual going on. No one slithering around in a trench coat. No odd clicking on his cellphone.

After fifteen or twenty minutes, Feinton reappeared, looking dour. "Mr. Cogan, I'm sorry, but it's not ready. It's not done yet. I was told it's not due until tomorrow and that you should come in late tomorrow afternoon. Around quarter to five or five. Would that be all right?"

"Well, the only problem," Cogan replied, "is that we are having a town meeting here on August 23, this coming Sunday. The title and summary have to be printed in the newspaper before we can begin circulating petitions. We had hoped to begin doing that at the Sunday meeting. If I can't get the notice back until late tomorrow, I can't get it down to the paper until Thursday. That would be cutting it very close. Would you mind explaining that to the town attorney and seeing if he might be able to get it back to us by at least four o'clock tomorrow?"

"I'll see. But it won't do any good," Feinton paused.

"I'll wait."

Another fifteen minutes passed before she returned.

"He said he can't promise anything before tomorrow afternoon at five."

"Can I speak with him for a moment?"

"I'm sorry. He's busy."

"It will only take a second."

"He's really tied up at the moment. Perhaps you can come back later."

"Can I make an appointment? What would be a good time?"

"I don't know. I don't keep his schedule."

"Does he have a secretary?"

"No. He keeps his own calendar."

"Can you ask him what time I should come back?"

At that, she got testy. Feinton really didn't want to go back into the office again. She really didn't want to. But Cogan insisted. As politely as possible. Reluctantly, she went back again. This time Cogan could hear at least part of what was being said.

"No. I'm not available. And don't come back in here again about this. Do you understand?" She did. Cogan was beginning to understand, too.

CHAPTER ELEVEN

NAIROBI

Katz knocked again. Harder this time. He had forgotten that Mark Fischer was probably still flipping back and forth between Fairview and Nairobi time. He undoubtedly had a serious case of jet lag and was probably sound asleep. He came to the door bleary eyed and looking exhausted.

"Paul," he groaned, "what brings you here in the middle of the night? How are you?"

"Sorry, Mark, I forgot what time you were on. I can come back."

"No, no." Fischer replied. "Come in, come in. What's up?"

After fifteen minutes or so of small talk, Katz finally got to the point. "Actually, Mark," he said, "the reason I'm here is that I'd like to talk to you. I need—we need—your help."

"What is it?"

"Have you heard about this Sean Cogan initiative business?"

"Somebody mentioned it to me in passing yesterday, but I don't know much."

"Do you know Sean Cogan?" asked Katz.

"Not really. I know he went to Fairview High long before I did. Tell me what the whole thing is about."

For the next twenty minutes Katz went through the entire story.

About the initiative, the reasons behind it, the meeting at the mayor's office, Partida's sledge hammer approach to fighting the initiative, Katz's disagreement with Partida, and so on.

"You're absolutely right, Paul," Fischer broke in, "you have to take this on in a completely honorable and above-board way. The high road. No dirty tricks. No slimy tactics or you'd play right into their hands. This initiative could pose a huge problem. I can just imagine the reaction in Kenya, hell, in a good part of Africa, if the initiative passes, or even comes close. A small town in America slamming government and corporate corruption? Voting for its independence? It could have real consequences. You're going to have to run a smart campaign against this. Really smart."

"**We** have to run a smart campaign."

"Paul, I can't... I have to get back to... I have obligations to my students."

"Mark, you have to do this. You have to help. We need you to help."

"Paul...'

"This is a big deal, Mark, you said so yourself. You're on summer break now, aren't you?"

"Yes, but..."

"When does school start up again?"

"The first week in September."

"You can go back early if you have to, but if you could stay through November tenth, through the election, you could see this thing through. I'm telling you, we can't leave the opposition in the hands of people like Partida. He's a complete dumbbell. No judgment. No tact. No common sense. But he's the mayor. He's the damn mayor. He's going to be visible in this. We need to put this together ourselves; if we don't, God only knows what might happen. We'll have the opposition coming at us from all sides."

"I don't know how I could do it, Paul, I really don't."

"Just think of it as though you got sick, or as though some emergency came up, and you couldn't travel. This really is an emergency."

"You really think this vote is going to take place?"

"I do. And God knows what could happen. A lot of people are really pissed off at Washington.

"I... I guess I could see if maybe one of my colleagues could fill in for a couple of months. It would be hard. The school will probably be really upset with me. But I'll think about it. Let me think about it."

Paul could tell from the way Mark was looking at him that he had already made his decision. He was going to do it. He was going to do it for sure.

Two days later Fischer called to confirm. His mission work would have to be put on hold for a bit. This project was important. Too important to leave to the hands of people like Partida.

It had been days since he had last checked his email, and Cogan knew it was not going to be pretty. Sure enough, the inbox had become a small dumpster. How was it possible for so many people to set aside so much time to send out so much drivel to so many recipients? Electronic junk mail. Amazing. Delete. Delete. Delete. Delete. But once again, Cogan's electronic erasing was trumped by that miracle of nose-butting known as Internet relay chatting.Sure enough, Moe-zus was back. This time with a vengeance. Cogan clicked him on. It was like opening a pontification box.

"Since you have been away from your computer," Moe-zus began, "I trust that either God has already acted to remove you from the world you are trying to ruin or that you are away. Probably on a trip to Gamora. In eithar event, I hope you are having a miserabul time. How goes the heresy business?"

"Der's no money in it deese days," Cogan replied. "All of da shakedowns has been taken over by your perverted, sex-starved, malodorous, revival-tent ranting, trailer-park dwelling, scum-snake friends. And by da way, it's either, miserable, and Gomorrah.

"But I don't have time for this right now, so I'd appreciate it if you'd save your ranting for the coming glory days of the new inquisition. Your mullah clones need you to be at your fresh-faced, saintly smiling, finger-pointing best. Cheers, Sean."

"P.S. Malodorous means smelly."

The phone rang. It was Danielle. "I think you should be gearing up," she said.

"Mattington has been snooping around, talking to people. Asking questions about you."

"What kind of questions?" Cogan asked.

"Anything and everything. You need to be ready so you're not caught off guard."

"That's ok," Cogan replied. "I'm all set."

"One other thing," she added. "Mattington's not the only one that's been asking questions. Some guy was hanging out at the Depot yesterday. Too stiff looking to be a reporter, too straight looking to be a local. New jeans and t-shirt. Fortyish and uptight looking."

"What was he asking? Who was he talking to?"

"He talked to a lot of people. Same type of questions as Mattington, but no note pad. Either he has a very good memory or he was recording."

"It's started, Danielle," Cogan said. "Hold on. Here we go."

CHAPTER TWELVE

ODD LOOKING GUY

Jen was just hopping out of the shower. "I'm sorry," apologized Cogan, "I'll call back in a few minutes.

"No, no. It's okay. It's fine. In fact, I'm really glad it's you. There was an odd looking guy walking up and down my street an hour ago. Just strolling and peering around. No one ever walks down this street unless accompanied by a golden retriever. It's too curvy, too hilly. There's no sidewalk."

"Fortyish? New jeans and t-shirt? Uptight looking?"

"That's him," Jen replied. "How'd you know?"

"He's making the rounds. Flash him a smile, and wave the next time."

"Why?"

"For your dossier."

"Are you serious? Sean, are you really serious?"

"Yep," Cogan replied. "And you know what? Real spooks are way too professional to be so conspicuous. I think they want us to know they're there. They want to intimidate us. I'll be right over."

"Well, they're not going to intimidate me," Jen said. "I don't scare that easily. The creepy bastards."

"That's just another reason to be falling in love with you," he said.

"I know," Jen replied strongly. "You're hooked already. Not much of a struggle for such a big fish. But what should we do about the gumshoes? Pretty soon they'll be crawling in through the windows."

"Let's go for a hike," Cogan suggested. "I'll be there in ten minutes."

"My goodness! Ten Minutes!" she laughed. "I could never get dressed that quickly."

"See you in seven. I'll take a shortcut."

As he backed out of his driveway, Cogan stopped to check his oversized mailbox.

As usual, he hadn't checked it for several days, and it mimicked his piles of email. In addition to the usual stack of coupon books, sale announcements, brochures, and bills, a small package sat to the rear of the space. It had no return address. There was an enveloped taped to the outside. It had to be the package Giller had mentioned.

After opening and reading the note, Cogan had to catch his breath. He read it again. Then he pulled his car back up to the house, carried the package inside, put it down on the coffee table, and reread the note for the third time. He folded it, inserted it into one of the cookbooks adjacent to the counter, and opened the package. "Jesus," he muttered to himself. For a few minutes, he just sat there in silence. Then he reached for the phone to call Jen. All he said was that he was going to have to cancel. Something had come up. He had work to do.

The package Cogan had received from Giller came with strict instructions not to discuss the situation with anyone. The word anyone had been underlined. But it drove Cogan nuts to be keeping anything from Jen. And besides, he needed her advice. She had really good judgment, and he wanted her take on the situation. He knew he'd probably been warned to keep his mouth shut to avoid blowing things by yammering into a bug. That was the last thing Cogan wanted to do.

Then it came to him. He would simply communicate with Jen by writing everything down—not on his computer but in longhand. Then he would go over to Jen's house and show it to her. She would reply the same way, and then they would burn everything.

It was ridiculous, and Cogan felt like a bit player in a low-budget spy film. But he did it. After following the instructions in the package to a tee, he sat down and started composing. For over an hour, he wrote page after page. He explained why he was putting everything in writing and laid out everything about the package he had just received. He warned Jen that they were probably under heavy surveillance and that their conversations were probably being recorded. He wrote and wrote until he finally got it all down. Twenty-six pages. His hand and fingers ached. My God, he thought. It felt like he was living in a police state.

He gathered the thick stack of paper, shook his cramping hand, jumped in his car, and headed for Jen's. The house was dark, the garage was closed and the front door was locked. Cogan called Jen on her home phone. No answer. On her cellphone. No answer. That wasn't like her. But there was nothing Cogan could do but sit in his car and wait. And while he waited, his mind played tricks on him. He began to worry about whether something might have happened to her. Could she have been abducted? Had she have been in an accident? Was she being held some-place? Interrogated? Minutes dragged on for hours. He tried calling her phones again. Nothing. He sat there in silence in the dark. Finally, he decided to just break in. Maybe he could find a hint of what was going on.

He grabbed his papers and stumbled in the dark toward the side of the house, tripping over a stone monk and crashing against a pine tree. As he wrestled to pry open a sliding glass door, he set off a burglar-alarm that accompanied its siren with a blinding overhead spotlight. Thankfully, Jen's car suddenly appeared. She quickly deactivated the alarm that was screaming, illuminating half the block, and waking up all of her neighbors using a remote.

"Hi!" She laughed. "What are you doing here? I just saw a hilarious movie.

"Shhhhh," cautioned Cogan leaning toward her car, more relieved than he could possibly say.

"Shhhhh???" Jen replied, thinking he was kidding. "You've just woken up half of Northern California, and you say, 'Shhhhh?'"

"Shhhhh," Cogan repeated, holding his index finger to his lips and motioning her to go inside. She rolled her car into the garage, then walked around and gingerly unlocked her front door, turning on the kitchen lights as she ushered Cogan forward. Laying his papers out on the kitchen table in front of her, Cogan again held his finger to his lips.

After carefully scanning the twenty-six pages, Jen stood up, walked over to a corner desk, and returned with a pen. She wrote for twenty or thirty seconds, reviewed her work, and then handed the sheet to Sean. Squinting and straining as he stared at the page, Cogan, giving up, finally mouthed the words "I can't read what you've written."

CHAPTER THIRTEEN

BACK TO TOWN HALL

The next day, Cogan showed up at the town hall at 4:00 p.m. just in case the paperwork was ready. It wasn't. Cogan had already spoken to Gerard Lawton, the publisher of the Fairview Post, himself an outspoken opponent of the way things were going in Washington. Lawton had promised to keep a slot open for the notice of title and summary. He would stay late, if necessary, to get it in on time.

Creswell hid in his office until 4:58. Finally he emerged briefly and presented some papers to Ms. Feinton. He then turned on his heel—without looking up or saying a word—retreated to his office. Feinton glanced at the sheet, smiled, and handed a copy of it to Cogan. When Cogan read it, he couldn't believe what he was reading. In large bold type were the words: "Unconstitutional. Initiative Application Denied."

Cogan was floored. Petty bureaucrat! Who the hell did he think he was?

Feinton didn't waste any time. "I'm sorry, Sir," she said, "It's five o'clock. We have to close. I'll have to ask you to leave the building."

"Wait a second," Cogan said. "I have to speak with Mr. Creswell about this."

"I'm sorry, Sir," she replied, "He's gone for the day."

"But I just saw him walk into that office."

"I'm sorry," Feinton repeated, "he's gone for the day."

"Can I make an appointment for tomorrow?"

"I'm sorry, Sir..."

Remembering, Cogan mimicked the words with Feinton, in unison.

"Mr. Creswell," they said together, "keeps his own calendar."

Feinton didn't think the impromptu duet was very funny. You could tell by her scowl. "Sir?"

"I know, I know," anticipated Cogan. "It's five o'clock, the building is closed, and I have to leave."

Cogan sat in the parking lot, reading the words on the sheet that had been given to him. "Unconstitutional. Initiative Application Denied." He hadn't expected that. The town attorney's actions could have the effect of derailing the entire effort. There could be no publication in the newspaper until there was a notice of title and summary to publish. Without it, they could not launch their signature drive.

Cogan slumped in his car, trying to figure out what to do. What was going on? It was unlikely that the town attorney was simply acting on his own. Higher ups had to be involved. Members of the town council. Maybe even the mayor. Jen would know. Cogan picked up his phone and started dialing. Just then, the rear door of the building opened, and a preoccupied-looking William Creswell emerged and bounded down the steps.

"Excuse me. Mr. Creswell..." Cogan called as he got out of his car.

"I'm sorry," Creswell replied, "I don't have time to... you'll have to make an appointment."

"Well, I'd like to make it right now then. Look, I just want to know what's going on here and..."

"I'm sorry," Creswell punted, "I don't have my calendar. It's in my office. And I have to be getting home. I'm late as it is." Without another word, Creswell got in his car, locked the door, waved Cogan away, started the engine, and backed up with a jump.

How could he be late? He'd left the office practically at the stroke of five. Creswell accelerated out of the lot, leaving Cogan standing there with his mouth open.

Cogan dialed Jen's cell number again. She picked up on the first ring. "What's up? How'd it go?"

Jen shifted into lawyer mode as Cogan conveyed the story. "I know Creswell," she said. "He's a pitiful little shit. I know what to do. I've got access to Lexus. Come on over with the papers he gave you. We'll be in front of the PJ first thing in the morning."

CHAPTER FOURTEEN

JUDGE CYNTHIA DAVIS

Cogan started his car and headed over to Jen's house. On the way he detoured by the Fairview Post to let Gerard Lawton know what had occurred. He thanked Lawton for staying late, apologized for wasting his time, and told him they planned to go to court in the morning.

"I'll be there," replied Lawton.

Jen, Cogan, and Lawton were all up early the following morning. They sat outside of Judge Davis's courtroom. When her clerk arrived, Jen handed him a stack of papers formally requesting issuance of an alternative writ of mandate. The proposed writ ordered the town of Fairview to provide Cogan with the notice of title and summary required under the elections code. The clerk disappeared into Judge Davis's chambers.

Twenty minutes later, Judge Davis directed the clerk to contact Creswell and have him report to her court within the hour.

Creswell hadn't counted on that. Not at all. He scooped up some irrelevant papers, threw them into his briefcase as props, and headed out the door, sweat gathering on his furrowed brow.

Judge Davis, a Harvard Law grad, looked every bit the part of the smart no-nonsense judge she was. Although known for her patience with the attorneys appearing before her, she had little tolerance for incompetence. She took the bench as the court reporter assumed her post in the mostly empty courtroom, wished everyone a good morning, and sat there scrutinizing Jen's moving papers, glancing from time to time at those seated before her. Finally, she spoke. "Mr. Creswell," she said, "Did you refuse to issue the title and summary for this proposed ballot initiative on the grounds that you believed the initiative to be unconstitutional?" "Yes, Your Honor, Creswell said, "I did."

"And by what authority did you do so."

"Well," replied Creswell, "by my authority as town attorney. This so-called ballot proposition is borderline seditious."

"Are you aware, Sir, of the constitutional concept known as the separation of powers?"

"I'm familiar with the term, Your Honor," he said, "but I confess that I am not an expert in constitutional law."

"Apparently not," Judge Davis said, raising her left eyebrow about an inch higher than the right. "Please understand that you, as the town attorney of Fairview, have not been appointed to serve as an initiative czar. Judges decide constitutional issues. Not town lawyers. Judges are part of the judicial branch of government. You are not a judge. Let me ask you this, Mr. Creswell. Before you declared this initiative to be unconstitutional, did you receive any authority to do so from any elected members of the town council?"

"No, Your Honor," Creswell stated, thinking to himself that the mayor was the mayor, not a council member.

"How about the mayor?" Davis followed up. "What's the mayor's name?"

"Partida, Your Honor, James Partida. But aren't my conversations with the mayor attorney-client privileged?"

"You just waived the privilege by your answer to my last question," Judge Davis pointed out.

God, thought Jen, Davis is one bright jurist.

"I'd rather not say," Creswell replied.

"I am ordering you to answer my question."

"Ah, well, I don't exactly recall the exact conversation."

"You did talk to him? About the initiative?"

"Generally."

"Did you discuss with him the idea of refusing to approve the initiative by finding it to be unconstitutional?"

"I don't recall, exactly, Your Honor."

"Think hard, Mr. Creswell. We'll wait."

Creswell's eyes darted about nervously. He was trapped. Not only that, but he suddenly remembered that the mayor voted as a member of the council. He had lied to Judge Davis in saying he hadn't discussed this with any members of the town council. Damn it. He didn't want to get himself in any more trouble.

"Yes, I remember now. We did discuss the unconstitutionality issue. Generally."

Jen had to muster all her self-control to avoid bursting into laughter. She dared not make eye contact with Cogan or the two of them would lose it.

"And did you discuss, generally, the effect that your actions would have on delaying the publication of the initiative and on the petition process?"

"Generally... yes. I guess we did. Generally."

"And did you also talk about taking other actions aimed at delaying the process or at keeping this initiative off the ballot?"

"Such as what, Your Honor?"

"Good question, Mr. Creswell. You tell me."

"There may have been some general discussion about that subject, possibly, but I don't recall just, you know, just exactly what that was." Lawton was writing furiously.

"Mr. Creswell, I want to make this very clear. As town attorney, you have every right to challenge the constitutionality or legality of this or any initiative. But you must do so in court, not in some back room at your town hall. And I'll tell you something else: as long as I am the presiding judge in this county, you will face a very difficult burden of proof in attempting to block voters from voting. On anything. *Anything*. Do I make myself clear, Sir?"

"Yes, Your Honor," Creswell said, suddenly remembering why he had decided, long ago, to stay out of courtrooms.

"One last thing. I am ordering you to provide a copy of this transcript to the mayor and to the town council. You will do so promptly. Understood?" "Yes."

"All right. I am finding that you and very possibly Mayor Partida may well have attempted to delay and/or to deny the right of the people of Fairview to exercise their right to vote on this matter. I am granting petitioner's alternative writ of mandate, and I am ordering you to provide the notice of title and summary required by the election code to the initiative's proponents no later than 2 p.m. tomorrow afternoon. Is there anything further?"

There wasn't.

As Judge Davis gathered her papers and departed for her chambers, Gerard Lawton, pen in hand, approached Creswell. "Can I ask you a few additional questions about all of this?" he asked.

"I don't have anything further to say," grunted Creswell.

"I'm just trying to give you an opportunity to comment on some of the issues that have been raised here," Lawton pressed. "Is this the only time you have tried to keep an initiative off the ballot by declaring it unconstitutional?"

"I have nothing further to say."

"Did Mayor Partida contact you about this, or did you alert him?"

"I have nothing further to say."

"What is your political party affiliation? What is your registration?" "I have nothing further to say."

"Are you concerned that your actions will help the proponents of this initiative to mobilize support?"

Creswell said nothing.

"Do you plan to appeal Judge Davis's order? Are you going to ask for a stay on the writ?"

That was an interesting question. It hadn't occurred to Creswell until then, but he could cause further delay in the publication and petition gathering process by simply seeking an appellate stay of Judge Davis's ruling. That would have the effect of putting her order on hold pending a decision by a court of appeals on the issue of whether Creswell's actions had, in fact, exceeded his authority. This question, he would go ahead and answer.

"We may very well do so." he said. The instant the words left his mouth, Creswell knew he should have stayed silent.

"But isn't it likely that doing so would just pour oil on the fire?"

"I have no comment."

"Whose decision is it whether to appeal or not?"

"I have nothing more to say."

"Are you at all concerned that you may have risked your job given possible public reaction to what you have done? Are you concerned about how the town council or the mayor's office will respond to the transcript you've been ordered to give them?"

Creswell was back in silent mode.

"How long have you been town attorney? What did you mean when you said that you didn't consider yourself an expert in constitutional law? Doesn't someone in your position have to have some expertise in constitutional law? Do you consider the concept of separation of powers to be a complicated concept, or is it fairly basic?"

Silence.

"Did you actually believe you were within your rights to refuse to allow this initiative to go on the ballot? Or did you just think you could get away with what you did, whether you were within your rights, or not?"

More silence.

"Did you discuss this with anyone besides Mayor Partida? Anyone at all?"

"Look, I was just doing my job. Okay? Like you do yours. Now if you don't mind, I have things to do. You are blocking the door, and I would appreciate it if you would just step aside."

"Certainly," Lawton said.

As Creswell headed for the exit, Cogan couldn't help himself, "I guess the appointment I was asking for won't be necessary," he grinned. "Never mind."

Creswell didn't respond. He was in a hurry.

As Cogan, Jen, and Lawton walked down the courthouse steps Cogan turned to Jen. "You were brilliant!" he smiled.

"I didn't say anything. Not a word."

"Exactly. You crushed the opposition without firing a shot."

Lawton laughed.

"Thank you," Jen smiled. "You can buy me lunch."

Cogan asked Lawton if he would join them.

"I'd like to," he said, taking out his cellphone and punching in a number, "I've got some questions for the two of you, as well. But I've got some work to do first."

Driving back to town hall, Creswell decided to take a few minutes to collect his thoughts and do a bit of preliminary legal research before calling Partida with the bad news. Unfortunately, that idea turned out to be yet another in his growing string of bad judgments. As a result of Creswell's delay, Lawton got to Partida first. So by the time Creswell phoned him, Partida was already midway through tearing the draperies off his living-room windows. To characterize him as being in a rage would be a serious understatement.

"I should have known better than to listen to you. You said you knew just what to do, that you had everything under control. Horseshit! Creswell. You are an idiot. And now you will be making *me* look like an idiot. Damn it. I am the mayor! I was planning to run for the State Assembly. And now I'm going to be seen as some kind of slime bucket. God damn it!"

Creswell just let Partida go on. And on. He knew how to handle screaming maniacs. He was married to one. He had learned, long ago, to simply hold the phone far enough away from his ear that he couldn't make out what was being said but could still hear the noise. That way, he wouldn't find himself baited into responding but also wouldn't be accused of not listening once the yelling had stopped. It was like watching a car running out of gas, sputtering and bouncing around until it came to rest.

After about fifteen minutes, Partida shut up. Creswell felt like asking, "Are you done?" but he knew that would just inflame Partida and elicit a rewind. Instead he threw Partida a distraction biscuit. "Sir, what if we appeal? What if we ask for a stay of Judge Davis's order and file an appeal on the merits?"

Partida released his grasp on the draperies. "Hmmmm," he said in a perfectly calm voice. It was as though he had already forgotten the ranting diatribe he had just completed. "Well," he said, rubbing his chin, "let's think about it this time. How would that work?"

"Well, I've actually already looked into that a little bit. We would file an appeal of

Judge Davis's ruling seeking a kind of emergency hearing before the State Court of Appeal. There are numerous different three-judge panels, any one of which could wind up hearing our request. Depending on the panel we happen to draw, we might well find ourselves before much more sympathetic judges than Davis. As part of our appeal, we would be asking for a stay, delaying the enforcement of

Judge Davis's order until the appellate court had a chance to consider the matter.

Even if we were to lose, we could then file a further appeal with the State Supreme Court, and then beyond that, even to the U.S. Supreme Court. Now, how do you think the types of judges that have been appointed to the U.S. Supreme Court over the past twenty years would react to all of this? Wham. In the meantime, win, lose, or draw, no title and summary. It might be somewhat expensive to do this, but it would give us three more bites of the apple. And to paraphrase a famous lawyer from the dusty annals of legal legendry, "If you want a de-lay, you just have to pay'."

"What?"

"Nothing. It was nothing."

"Hummm," Partida said for the second time in less than a minute. Creswell knew that meant he was thinking.

The next day's *Fairview Post* front-page was enough to get the attention of even the most casual observer: "Judge Slams Fairview Officials: Rules mayor, town attorney ignored constitutional guarantees, conspired to keep anti-government measure off ballot." The article went on for two full pages and quoted Judge Davis at length, as well as noting the non-comments and more voluble but still banal responses of Creswell, Partida, and others.

The article also reported on the reactions of local residents to Judge Davis's order, like those of Randy Walters, who said, "I don't know why local officials think they have the right to keep something off the ballot. They might not like this initiative. I may not like it either—I don't know enough about it at this point—but, really, who do they think they are to prevent us from voting on something? It seems pretty underhanded to me."

Katz, who had been out of town on business for two days, spotted the story in a stack of just-delivered newspapers piled up at the Fairview Market. He couldn't believe his eyes. This was exactly what he had predicted. Goddamn Partida. He was an arrogant, simple-minded, dimwit. "Cornell, my ass," Katz muttered. Partida operated like a kindergarten dropout.

CHAPTER FIFTEEN

STRONG REACTIONS

Bruno listened carefully to Chino Vasquez and Chuck McMann, the two agents he had assigned to the project. He had a printout of the newspaper article in front of him. Although their workup was far from complete, both Vasquez and McMann had strong reactions.

"This guy Cogan," Vasquez said, "is popular and bright. So is the woman, Renton—the lawyer—who appears to be Cogan's girlfriend. I think it would be a mistake to concentrate our efforts entirely on fact gathering. We need to be more proactive. At first blush, the idea of a tiny town voting for its independence seems absurd, but if we just sit back collecting information and letting things move forward on their own, there's no predicting how this will all play out or what the spillover effects might be." Bruno rubbed his stubbly face.

"I agree with Chino," McMann said. "I don't think we should just stand on the sidelines waiting for things to unfold. I think we need to be more proactive in dealing with this."

"Proactive." Bruno knew exactly what they meant. Some agents always favored simple solutions. "I don't know," replied Bruno. "I would bet that not many people will actually vote for this stupid thing. I don't think most folks are anywhere near that pissed off. And besides, towns can't just up and declare their independence. That's ridiculous. This is all going to be a big waste of time.

"And what could we do about Cogan anyway? Yank him off the street? Waterboard him? It's too late for that. Following this article, he's become too high profile. If we go after him, he and his touchy-feely lawyer girl-friend would just file a stack of lawsuits and follow up with a dozen depositions and a twohundred-page document request. God knows where that would wind up. With all of the activist judges running around, who knows what they'd order us to turn over? We'd have to really crank up the paper shredders. And we need copies of a lot of the stuff we'd have to be destroying. It's just too risky."

Vasquez shot a subtle glance at McMann, as though to say, "What did I tell you?"

Bruno didn't notice. "They may not even get the necessary signatures to put this thing on the ballot," he continued. "And if they do, we'll just bring in Howie Ratson. We'll give him whatever he needs, and he'll just bury them. The initiative will go up in smoke. We can take care of Cogan and his girlfriend later, if we even have to at that point. But for now, I think we should let them spin their wheels."

McMann wasn't satisfied. He wanted to put Cogan out of commission. "Taking care of him and his girlfriend later on is all well and good," he said. "But the longer we sit back and allow them to run around stirring people up, the bigger the problem we're going to have. Maybe our options are limited, but there are things we can do."

"What do you recommend?"

"Let me think about it a bit more," McMann demurred. "I'll report back in a week."

"Okay," Bruno relented. "But keep me posted. And don't do anything significant unless I okay it. In writing. Got it?"

"All right," McMann lied. In truth, McMann had already done more than just think about it. But there was no need for Bruno to know that.

McMann simply wanted to have more leeway, more authority. But Bruno was not about to agree to any such thing. McMann's experience and track record fell far short of his ambition, and he had to be kept on a short leash. The whole situation was going to be continuously reported to some very highly placed individuals. Bruno would oversee this. And his name, not McMann's, would be on the bottom line of every memo.

Suddenly, Bruno interrupted the meeting to glance down at the vibrating phone attached to his belt. The damned thing always made him have to go to the bathroom. "I'm sorry," he said, I have to take this call. We'll have to continue this discussion later."

"Damn it," Bruno muttered. "Why did they put the fucking bathroom way around in the back?" It wasn't easy to walk casually past dozens of nodding subordinates grinning like an idiot while you were struggling with all your being to avoid peeing in your pants.

CHAPTER SIXTEEN

TITLE AND SUMMARY

"Jimmy?" the voice said.

"Katz." Partida muttered under his breath. He could tell who was on the line before the son of a bitch even said his name. He had known the call would be coming, and he'd been waiting for it like a patient waits for a colonoscopy. "Hello,

Paul."

"Hello, Jimmy," Katz said. He wasn't even trying to mask his condescension.

"Jimmy," he intoned. It was the third time Katz had called him Jimmy in less than

a minute. "From my reading of the screaming headline in this morning's paper, it would seem that you and your friend Creswell really kind of fucked up here. Big time."

Katz's tone was as impatient and insulting as a human voice could be.

"It's not the best morning I've ever had," Partida muttered.

"You know, I do have to say I told you so. Because, well, because I DID. And, frankly, even I didn't think anything THIS bad could happen with the approach you insisted on taking. But it did, Jimmy, it surely did. A court order? A constitutional woodshed whipping by a highly respected superior court judge? The idea that opponents of this measure are trying to block residents from even voting on it? A newspaper story that will no doubt wind up as a campaign hit piece? Jimmy, you could not possibly have done a bigger favor for the proponents of this harebrained proposition.

"You have given these people two things they would never otherwise have been able to get. One, sympathetic credibility with a large number of people who wouldn't otherwise have given them the time of day, and two, early-stage publicity that could continue to grow. So what are you planning on doing next?"

"Well, one possibility that we've been kicking around," Partida answered, "is appealing Judge Davis's decision."

"You're thinking of appealing the decision. Is that so? And for what reasons? To take the chance that three appellate judges might make things even worse for us? To bolster the argument that proposition opponents are using legal delaying tactics to keep this initiative off the ballot? To set off a new round of hideous publicity? To create even more sympathetic credibility for the proponents? To hand them an even bigger organizing tool? To assure that people who would never otherwise have signed the petition to place this on the ballot will not only sign but will volunteer to gather signatures from their neighbors? Let's see now, what have I missed? What a terrific idea! Appeal Judge Davis's decision. Did Mr. Creswell come up with that, Jimmy, or did you think of it all by yourself?"

Katz was a sarcastic, pompous, nasty little ass. "I will take your objections under advisement," Partida said, "and will convey them to the council when we go into executive session."

"Executive session?" scowled Katz. "You're actually planning on discussing all of this behind closed doors, with the public and the media excluded. Is that what you're saying?"

"The council always discusses legal matters in executive session. Always. For one thing, although I am not personally an attorney, it is my understanding that the confidentiality of discussions with our lawyer would be waived if the conversations were to take place in a public meeting. We can't be having strategy sessions in public. That would be crazy."

"No,' replied Katz, "that's not what would be crazy. What would be crazy would be to slam the door on the people of Fairview on an issue that you, Jimmy, have already turned into a ludicrous fiasco. And what would be even crazier would be to roll the dice with regard to how the news media would react to being locked out of the room."

Why was it that Katz always seemed to think he was the brightest light in the night? By the time this was all over, Partida would teach him a lesson or two. "I've got to go," Partida said. "I have things to do." Partida probably had lots of things to do. Starting with throwing down a quick pick-me-up before lunch. After all, it was getting late. It was already almost ten thirty in the morning.

Half an hour later, Partida, his pick-me-up in hand, thought about Katz's concerns about going into executive session to discuss what to do. Maybe the pompous bastard was actually right. Besides, Partida wasn't about to slide into the trap that awaited him if he guessed wrong. He would never be able to handle Katz's bitching and sermonizing if he called the council into executive session and it blew up in their faces.

Beyond that, Partida faced a serious timing problem. The town was under a court order to provide the title and summary documents by 2 p.m., less than two hours away. Unless Cresswell secured a stay before then, the town would be held in contempt if it failed to do as Judge Davis had ordered. That would be no laughing matter. A ruling of contempt could mean anything from the town's having to pay an embarrassing fine to Mayor Partida's having to spend a night in the county jail. Neither alternative was attractive. Especially not to a politician. And even if

Partida called an immediate emergency session and even if the council voted in favor of seeking a stay and filing an appeal, there simply wasn't enough time to complete that process plus obtain the stay before 2 o'clock.

Creswell, who had already prepared a rough draft of the title and summary, just in case, was awaiting his marching orders. If he got the go-ahead from Partida to issue the papers to Cogan, the proposition's supporters could begin gathering signatures on Monday. At least, thought Creswell, he had prevented the initiative's proponents from gathering signatures at the rally on the twenty-third. Partida walked over to Creswell's office, swallowed hard, and reluctantly gave him the go-ahead.

Shortly before the witching hour, the required documentation was hand delivered to Cogan's house. What the draftsmanship may have lacked in sophistication, it made up for in conciseness:

TITLE

Proposition A: Fairview Self-Rule/Independence Initiative.

SUMMARY

Proposition A seeks political independence for the Town of Fairview, free from governance by any outside entities. The initiative will give the power to the Town of Fairview, and its citizens, to ignore or disregard any laws or decisions by other political entities which, by majority vote, the citizens of Fairview deem to be unfair or immoral.

Cogan read the papers, thanked the messenger, and grabbed his phone. Jen's voice mail came on. It was the first time Cogan had ever heard it. "Hi. This is Jen. I'm sorry I missed your call. Please leave a message or else I'll worry that one of the government spooks in the ironed blue jeans who's been prowling around town asking questions about me has now started calling me at home. Ugh. Creepy. Namaste. Bye."

Cogan couldn't resist. He lowered his voice and replied, "Hello. This is Agent

Southwit. I can't leave my number because that violates agency protocol. But I hear you give fabulous massages, and God knows I need one. If you don't like my ironed jeans, I'll just leave them at the hotel and come over in a bath towel. But please answer the door quickly. I don't want to be written up for standing around in the street half naked waiting to get a shiatsu from someone I'm supposed to be tailing. Thank you and Namaste, yourself."

Cogan headed down to the Fairview Post and handed the title and summary to Lawson. Lawson read it, smiled, and handed it to an assistant. "Can you get this in the paper for a three-day starting tomorrow?" he asked.

"No problem," replied the assistant.

Right, thought Cogan. No problem.

CHAPTER SEVENTEEN

BILL CONNELLY CHECKS IN

It was a hot, late-August day. A large crowd started to gather in front of town hall at about noon. They came with cameras, bottled water, knapsacks, and small children. By the time 1 p.m. arrived, there was hardly any room left in front of the building or the surrounding street. Fortunately, Geoffrey and Danielle had made arrangements for a sound system with several speakers placed throughout the area. Two portable microphones were available for anyone who wanted to speak. The scene felt like a political rally, with one big exception: the atmosphere. There was no music, no light-hearted banter, and no air of frivolity. Just the low murmur of discussion and nervousness. Thanks to all the attention given to Judge Davis's order, news reporters and camera crews were out in force. Including, of course, Chris Mattington. Whatever happened today would be on the evening news and in the next day's papers.

Standing on the town hall steps, Cogan was flanked by Jen, Geoffrey, Ollie, and Danielle. "Try to talk in concise sound bites," Danielle said. "Rambling statements will just wind up on the cutting room floor." David Oster, standing toward the front, shot Cogan a thumb's up. He still thought it was all pretty wacky, but his definition of friendship didn't require a psychological litmus test. Cogan scanned the crowd for Giller but to no avail.

As his mind drifted, he thought about how odd it was to be finding himself standing there. He could be on his way to a ball game or heading off with Jen for an afternoon of cycling or hiking. Instead, he was launching a campaign to fire a broadside across the bow of those he believed had hijacked his country. Traitors camouflaged as patriots. Hypocrites, Goddamned hypocrites. Finally, he turned on his microphone. As the crowd settled down he took a deep breath, swallowed hard, and began.

"As I look out across this crowd and see so many of my friends and neighbors, I do so with a heavy heart. Like many of you I have deep roots in this community. I was born and raised not half a mile from this spot. And despite having traveled to many places far from home, this is the only place I would want to spend my life. Here, with the people I love." Absently, he cast a glance at Jen.

"For most of my life, I have felt these same feelings about America. Even at this moment, in fact, I cannot even utter the word *America* without feeling a surge of emotion welling up from a very deep place in my heart. But it is not the word that causes that feeling to surface. It is not the mountains or the majesty or the fruited plains. Or the songs about them. It is something very different and a lot more important. It's about the promise written to future generations in the words of our forefathers, that ours would be a government of, by, and for the people. That simple promise was the very cornerstone of our democracy.

"But that promise has been broken. Shattered. Today, our nation is awash with corrupt corporate leaders and crooked politicians. We have a government that is oppressing people, suppressing freedom of speech and assembly, spying on its citizens, and burdening them and future generations with huge financial obligations that are often being incurred simply to fund absurd spending projects proposed by members of Congress to pay off the billionaires who contribute millions to them. Paying for boondoggles that are useless to the people instead of funding the things we really need. The system is truly broken. And it is beyond our power to fix it. No reform movement, no new political party, no election can change this. Our congress and courts have decreed that paying off politicians with vast sums of money is a protected right akin to freedom of speech. Therefore, bribery and pay-offs are not only legal in our Country, they are constitutionally protected. Short of amending the Constitution – which could never happen - nothing can be done about it. We are talking about embedded systemic corruption on a grand scale. And payoff immunities are not limited to U.S. billionaires. In the Citizens United Case the Supreme Court opened the graft floodgates to foreign billionaires as well. To toxic chemical polluters, child labor predators, drug lords, slave owners...just name it!

"I have concluded that the only recourse we have, the only power we have left really, is the power to say NO. Not in my name. The initiative that we – myself, Jen, Danielle, Geoffery, Ollie and the many volunteers that are signing up by the hour – are asking you to support and vote for, empowers Fairview to make every peaceful effort necessary to establish our independence of our town. Our unwillingness to continue to be a part of this. To go to the polls in November and cast a vote that will be heard across the land—a vote that says, loudly and clearly, 'Enough. We have had it.' A vote that says that the folks who are running things may control the system, but they don't control us—the people of Fairview."

Scattered applause erupted amid nervous silence. "I believe, given what has happened to our country, that this is the most effective thing, in fact the only thing, we can do to preserve democracy and restore our rights.

"Perhaps you agree; perhaps you disagree. But we are here today to discuss it in the great tradition of the town meetings that have been held in our communities since the 1600s. We have microphones we can pass around. Just raise your hand if you'd like to speak."

For what seemed like several minutes, people just glanced around at each other, looking uncomfortable and waiting for someone else to get things started. Finally a middle-aged man toward the front raised his hand and was given a microphone.

"My name is Willard Sutter," he said, "and I'm sorry, Mr. Cogan, but to be quite candid, I think you are an egomaniac and a fool…"

Cogan, cut him off. "Thank you, Willard," he said with condescension, "and to what may I credit your thoughtful critique?" A nervous snicker rolled over the assembled crowd.

"Our country is as great as it always has been," Sutter replied. "And our government, institutions, and public officials are as honorable as any in the world."

"Is that so?" Cogan shot back. Jen squirmed, worried that his well-known temper was about to erupt. She could imagine his response as being *why don't you just stick it up your wazoo, Willard?* But Cogan didn't bite. Instead, he simply looked at his critic as though he was bored out of his mind.

"Yes, it is true" Sutter replied. "We are facing some big challenges. But this is a time for us to pull together—not be torn apart. You can make up whatever kind of crazy stories and whatever kind of paranoid reality you want to, Mr. Cogan, but the bottom line, Sir, is that you are just a spoiled rich guy. These things you are saying are exaggerations and distortions, and you are basically full of it. America is seen as a guiding light and a beacon of hope all over the world. And if you don't love this great country and everything it represents, then you should just get your ungrateful ass the hell out." A few cheers and whoops broke out.

Cogan started to respond but was interrupted by an elderly man with a thick head of white hair and a booming voice. "My name is Morgan Feldman," he said loudly, "and at eighty-three, I pretty near qualify as a Founding Father myself." The crowd laughed. Feldman was a well-known and beloved character around town.

"I have lived here in Fairview my whole life, Mr. Sutter, and although I have never to my knowledge even seen you before and don't know who you are or where you come from. I can tell you that Mr. Cogan is a good, decent, and honorable man. Moreover, he is right about everything he just said, and I am proud to live in the same town with him. And in my humble opinion, Mr. Sutter, it is not Mr. Cogan who is full of it; it's you. You are the one who is full of it. And the people who should get out are not the ones like Mr. Cogan, but the ones like you, Mr. Sutter. In fact," declared Feldman, waiving a ten-dollar bill in the air, "I'm going to start a collection right now to put you on the next boat to Beijing. And good riddance." The fact that Feldman was usually a soft spoken and gentlemanly sort of person, made his outburst even more potent.

Suddenly, the crowd came alive. "Sean," Feldman continued, "some people will try to discourage you. They will call you names like this stranger Sutter just did. But don't pay attention to them at all. We are smart, commonsense voters in this town. Most of us are going to know what to do on this proposition. You can bet on it."

A woman with long graying hair was standing off to the side with a fourteen- or fifteen-year-old boy. Getting a microphone, she said there was something she didn't understand: "I don't understand how we can just have a vote and declare our independence. How can we do that? Isn't that what the South tried to do in the Civil War? How are the state and federal governments going to respond?"

Jen, who apparently knew the woman, responded. "We don't know exactly what will happen, Janet. The ballot proposition simply says that we are declaring our independence. From the corruption, the pay-offs, the destruction of our civil liberties, the massive deficits, the bloated bureaucracy, the lack of accountability and all the rest. And as to any law, regulation or court decision that we deem unjust, unfair or immoral, we reserve the right to vote it down. If that happens, the people of Fairview, with the support of our town as a government entity, may simply refuse to abide by it. We don't know exactly what will occur. And we certainly aren't talking about initiating some kind of civil uprising or insurrection, or guerilla movement, as in various places around the world. Nothing like that. We are adamantly opposed to that. We are talking about non-violence. Thoreau, Gandi, Rosa Parks, Reverand King... We are simply saying that our government is not what it was promised to be. An oppressive, dominating system has taken root. We are saying that we cannot—and will not— continue to be a part of this. Speaking for myself," Jen continued, "I don't care how the government responds. I want to do this simply because it's the right thing to do." That hit a nerve and a loud cheer went up from a small portion of the audience.

"What about the financial issues?" asked a man who looked like an accountant in his button-down blue oxford shirt and khaki shorts. "How would Fairview be able to make it on its own?"

Ollie and Geoffrey, who were standing alongside Cogan on the landing in front of the building's massive front door, were ready. "Actually," Ollie answered, "we might do quite well on that score. First, I would expect tourism to go through the ceiling. People from all over would flock to Fairview to see what is happening here. Maybe we could start our own banking system—like in the Netherlands

Antilles, the British Virgin Islands, Lichtenstein, and other places. In fact, I wouldn't be surprised to see a considerable amount of money flowing in from all over, both in and out-of-state."

Scattered snickers rolled across the gathering as the local residents considered the prospect of a burgeoning banking and trust-management industry fueled by wealthy neighbors parking their assets in onshore/ offshore trust accounts domiciled just down the block. "We're researching this right now," continued Ollie, "and may have some information soon."

"How are we going to protect ourselves?" asked a voice from some-where in the middle of the crowd."

Cogan couldn't resist. "Maybe we'll enter into a mutual defense treaty with Martinique," he said with a straight face. The crowd laughed again.

"String bikinis for uniforms," Danielle added.

A familiar face that Cogan couldn't quite place reached for a micro-phone. "What's the deal with the newspaper article about the mayor?" the man asked. The article had already run Partida and Cresswell right through a wall; it was more than enough to have made the point. Cogan decided to avoid overkill. "A little handslapping lesson in constitutional law for His Honor and His Honor's counsel," Cogan replied. "The paper explains what happened better than I can."

A stocky, middle-aged guy who had been standing about twenty feet away, just kind of swaying back and forth, had heard enough He charged at Cogan, a silver object shining in his right hand. "Idiot," he screamed. He looked athletic, but Geoffrey, a tae kwon do black belt, was on him before he got close to Cogan. In a flash he had the guy on the ground with his forearm twisted grotesquely behind his neck. The silver object, which turned out to be a small switchblade, dropped to the ground. Three cops suddenly appeared from nowhere, and in less than thirty seconds, the whole incident was over. As the man was being hauled off, Cogan laughed at him. "Nice try, wimp. Can I keep the butter knife?"

The crowd, seeing Cogan's reaction went from stunned silence to nervous laughter. Cogan grinned and jumped back to the business at hand.

The discussion continued for another half an hour or so, but gradually the crowd dispersed. Soon only a handful of stragglers remained. All things considered, it had been a civil and productive meeting. Cogan was satisfied. Katz felt the same way. He had stood deep in the crowd with Mark Fischer by his side, the two of them taking it all in. The TV and radio stations, after hounding the cops for the name of the assailant, stuck around for one-on-one interviews with Cogan and with some of the people who had spoken up during the meeting.

That night and the next day, the press hit. It started with the broadcast media. Local radio and television stations. All of them aired major stories, many leading with the attack on Cogan and his reaction. Some of the network affiliates beamed footage to their New York and D.C. headquarters, and as a result, some stories aired elsewhere in the nation.

In an effort to gauge how the coverage might affect public opinion, Danielle did her best to catch as many of the segments as possible. All things considered, she was fairly satisfied with the way the whole thing was being played.

Mattington's article was typical of the print media's coverage. It went out on the wires and appeared Monday morning in hundreds of newspapers nationwide. It bore the headline: "Tiny Town May Seek Independence from U.S. 'Enough is Enough' Declares Initiative Proponent." It described Fairview as a small, pleasant, tree-lined town of some 13,000 people including 9,300 registered voters.

Mattington provided biographical details for Sean Cogan, whom he described as a disheartened American who had been pushed beyond his limits by what he considered grave threats to our most basic values as a nation. Going on to discuss Cogan's concerns, Mattington quoted the simple wording of the ballot proposition for which petitions were about to be circulated.

The article described the initiative process and how it worked and discussed whether a town like Fairview could actually declare its independence, and if so, what that would mean.

"Stranger things have happened," Mattington wrote, running through a litany of recent independence movements. "One can only speculate as to how state and federal officials might react. But for now, Cogan might have his hands full just in dealing with some of his neighbors. At Sunday's town meeting, one audience member called him an egomaniac, a fool, and a misguided, spoiled rich guy, and another tried to stab him with a small switchblade that Cogan jokingly characterized as a butter knife."

Mattington also described the reactions of Morgan Feldman and several other speakers. Mercifully, he left out Danielle's comment about the string-bikini uniforms. He touched only lightly on Ollie's "offshore" banking idea. "Stay tuned," the story closed, "this might get interesting."

Danielle told Cogan to expect inquiries from some of the local and national TV and radio talk shows. "Producers will start calling you, but let me deal with them. Just put recordings on your phones forwarding all media calls to me. I'll send out an email to the major players telling them to contact me with any questions or interview requests.

Cogan was skeptical. "Do you really think the big fish are going to have that kind of interest in this?"

"I've already got one of them on the hook," Danielle replied, "and you're going to love this. Bill Connolly's producer contacted me to say, quote-end quote, 'Connolly wants a piece of him while there are still pieces left.'"

"Connolly," laughed Cogan, "is the most popular looney in the Fox asylum. He really is a pompous ass. Did you set it up?"

"I did," smiled Danielle."

"I can't wait," Cogan replied. "I can't wait."

Chuck McMann hit the off button and tossed the remote across his blue-gray textured sofa. This was exactly what he'd been concerned about. Cogan was already getting network air time—and he wasn't coming across the way that Bruno had predicted. He wasn't being portrayed as the nut he was, but as a sincere, rational, relatively thoughtful guy. Once again, Bruno had ignored McMann's advice. Once again, Bruno had wimped out. The guy had been around for too long. He had gotten soft. CenTel needed to replace him with somebody more decisive, with somebody tougher. Somebody with cajones. With somebody like McMann.

The next day, Geoffrey, Danielle, Ollie, and half a dozen other volunteers set up card tables all over town. A poster-size blowup of the Fairview Post headline, "Judge Slams Fairview Officials," hung prominently from each table. In front of the Book Depot, on the sidewalk between the movie theatre and the French bakery, outside Safeway, and next to Angelo's Restaurant. They were there to hand out flyers, answer questions, and solicit petition signatures. They had no idea what kind of responses they were going to get. They assumed that emotions, pro or con, might well run high, and they were prepared for the worst.

But the worst did not happen. Instead of encountering strong emotions, they were met with exactly the opposite. A surprising number of people had either been to the town meeting or talked to someone who had. Most had read or heard about it in the media. It was amazing how quickly word had spread. One after the other, people stopped to talk. Conversations—for the most part calm, rational, conversations—took place. Small groups formed around the little tables. Even those strongly opposed to the initiative gathered to talk. And people signed. Some complained, but many signed. Not in vast numbers, not in droves, but they signed. By the end of the day, volunteers had gathered several hundred signatures.

While all of that was going on, Mayor Partida was doing some organizing himself. Along with Carl Sandgrow and Wilma Nolan, Partida put together a citizen's task force to campaign against the initiative, to raise money, to make public appearances, to generate media attention, to solicit anti-initiative endorsements, to rally the business community, and to coordinate with state and local patriotic organizations. He wanted to do everything he could to oppose a ballot initiative that would bring embarrassment and disgrace to Fairview. He wanted nothing to take place that would call into question the loyalty or patriotism of his fellow citizens. That could not happen. Not on his beat.

Partida wasn't having much trouble finding support for his organizing efforts. Both people he recognized and some whom he had never seen before were ready to join him. There were apparently a lot of people in town who wanted to stick an axe handle into Cogan's spokes. Some of them would have jumped at the opportunity to stick it somewhere else. Quite separate and apart from what Partida was doing, Paul Katz and Mark Fischer were also hard at work.

When Mayor Partida's secretary buzzed him to say that Howard Ratson was on the line, he thought she was kidding. Ratson's picture had been on the cover of numerous major news magazines as one of the savviest political operators in the Country. A heavyset, balding, confident, and supremely committed man, Ratson had managed campaigns and won elections that people said he could never win— often on behalf of candidates who weren't even close to being considered electable.

"Hello," Partida answered skeptically.

"Mr. Mayor," Ratson said, "how are you today? How's the weather up there?" It was him.

Mr. Mayor! That had a particularly impressive ring to it when it came from someone of Ratson's stature. "Fine, fine. I'm just fine," gushed Partida. "I'm honored to be speaking to you."

"The honor is mine. I've heard a lot about you—all of it good. I'm just calling to see if I can be of any help with this initiative business you're fighting."

"Well, you certainly can, Mr. Ratson."

"Please, just call me Howie."

"And James," Partida said.

"Thank you, James," Howie responded. "This initiative has piqued my interest because it's so odd that anyone could want to propose something like this. We're wondering if there isn't more here than meets the eye."

"We're"? thought Partida. Who was W*e're*?

"We're wondering what we can do. Of course, the print and broadcast media will be all over this, giving tons of free publicity to the whacko proponents of this thing. Even a close vote could cause problems, both here and abroad. And so although I'm sure that others are looking into the situation from a number of different angles, I just want you to know that I want to do to do whatever I can to help on the political front. To use whatever resources, I can to drive this proposition down."

"Do you have time to come out here?" asked Partida.

"That might not be the best way to go. The press would pick up on my involvement and that would give credibility to the proposition. I can send someone else—someone who won't be recognizable. My involvement should be sub rosa, so to speak, behind the scenes. Would that work?"

"Perfect," Partida said. "What exactly would you do?"

"Typical campaign stuff," Ratson chuckled. "Polling, focus groups, spin operations, voter education, coordination efforts, work with religious and other organizations, press stuff..." Ratson paused for a moment, as though he was trying to decide whether to say something or not and how to put it, "and opposition research."

"Opposition research?"

"Yes, and as a matter of fact, let me start with you. What can you tell me about this Cogan guy? We're going to need to hit him with whatever we can."

"So far as I know, he's just a rich guy who came home. Popular. Longtime local resident. He basically retired when his company was acquired by B of A. He fancies himself a patriot."

"A patriot?" Ratson spit out. "Some patriot. We need to dig up information on Mr. Cogan. I'm already on it from down here, but why don't you see what you can come up with locally."

"Like... personal stuff?"

"Right. See if there's any buzz about him. Drugs, sex, things he may have written, financial issues, past problems with the law. You can usually get good stuff from ex-girlfriends, ex-business partners, court records, lawsuits, depositions he may have given. Some people are going to be really pissed off at him for what he's doing. We need to find out who they are and what they might know. Or think they know. Just look into it. Quietly. Very quietly. And don't discuss me or my involvement with anyone. Not even Mary."

Mary was Partida's wife. Ratson had done his homework.

"And tell your secretary, the one who put my call through to you, that this was just a crank call from an old friend playing a joke on you."

"OK. A crank call. I get it, prevent rumors from starting. I'll tell her that as soon as

I hang up. "

"I'll have a fellow by the name of Bruno contact you. He's on another project right now, but it's closely related to this. He's very good. I'll talk to him and have him help out with the electoral part of this. He has a lot of political experience, and he's very bright. Just tell anyone who asks about him that he's just another volunteer. He'll be in touch within a few days."

"Thank you very much."

"Thank you. We're lucky to have you in your position as mayor, as the point man on this. If it weren't for you, the situation could spiral out of control. It could even spread to other places and really become a thorn in our sides. I'm looking forward to working with you. Talk to you soon, James."

"OK, Howie, talk to you soon." Partida hung up the phone with a glazed smile on his face. The idea that he was their point man was enough to take his breath away. *Howie,* he thought. He was calling Howard Ratson by his nickname. By the time all was said and done, this initiative could make him into a well-known figure in some very important places.

After less than a week of petitioning, Geoffrey was quite surprised. He had expected that it was going to take weeks of dedicated arm twisting to gather the 937 signatures needed to put the initiative on the November ballot. But the rapidly expanding group of volunteers had already gathered over two thousand names. That was a lot more than needed to cover likely challenges and invalidations. They carted the signatures down to the town clerk's office and submitted them for verification.

All things considered, Danielle reflected, gathering signatures had been a good experience, despite an obviously coordinated harassment campaign that had been initiated against them. On one occasion, a dozen or more anti-initiative protestors showed up at a petition site even before the volunteers had arrived. How they had learned the time, place, or other details was unknown. The protestors waved signs reading, "Traitor," "Shame," and Danielle's favorite, "Nothing is free—not even speech." Apparently the sign carriers were unaware of the irony of their message. Aside from that, and one egg-thrower with terrible aim, Danielle had no problems to report.

What was important was that the more time passed, the more interest was being expressed about the underlying issues. People were picking up on the excessive taxation issue. There was also a lot of talk about how passive people had become. Comparisons to the sixties were commonplace. "We wouldn't have put up with this nonsense for five minutes," announced one sixty-something-year-old in a suit and tie. "We would have been torching banks, organizing strikes and boycotts, and rioting in the streets." From the comments Danielle was hearing, it was becoming increasingly clear that a lot of people were starting to think about things that they hadn't thought about for a long time.

CHAPTER EIGHTEEN

SPEECHES

Chuck McMann had decided what to do on his own. He hadn't consulted with Bruno. Besides, he hadn't done anything irreversible. Not yet. McMann had just provided CenTel with an option. That was all. If Bruno put the axe to this, nobody would ever find out about it. No one had been caught, and Cogan was clueless. By the time he realized what had happened, it would be too late.

McMann sat in his car in a quiet corner of Fairview's Whole Foods parking lot and dialed Bruno's number. CenTel's policy was to leave no trail. Nothing related to security was put in writing. Certainly not things like this. He would just give Bruno a verbal report on the situation. Bruno would be upset that things had gone as far as they had without his specific approval, but so what? Something had to be done.

It was actually better for Bruno this way. If they'd been caught, McMann and Vasquez would have taken the hit themselves. There would have been no exposure up the chain. On the other hand, if they avoided detection and things worked out, Bruno, could later take the credit.

Paul Katz and Mark Fischer sat on a couple of chaise lounges on Katz's deck. While neither was an experienced campaign pro, they both had really solid instincts. They had rounded up a dozen or more volunteers to help and had divided tasks into six categories: press, endorsements, speaking engagements, fund raising, advertising, and getting out the vote. "Should we try to work with Partida and his people?" asked Fischer.

"I think," replied Paul, "that coordination should be minimal and very one-sided. We should tell them as little as possible about what we are doing and should try and find out as much as we can about what they are up to. I'm concerned about Partida's rather remarkable track record when it comes to screwing things up. In any event, he hates me." Paul continued, "You'll have to be in charge of him."

"OK," Fischer agreed. "I'll handle His Honor. I'll pay him a visit, flatter his ego, and try to keep current with what his people are doing."

With Partida, thought Paul, that would certainly be the best approach.

Over the next three weeks, Fischer made anti-initiative speeches to churches and business groups all over town. He called Cogan a fool, a spoiled rich guy, a naïve phony, and worse. "Tell me," Fischer railed to an overflow audience at St. Catherine's church hall, "why would any fair-minded person shun our nation's democratically elected leadership?" Harping on campaign finance, he asked, "Who is Sean Cogan to be telling the people of other states who they can and can't send to Congress? Who is he to be challenging the rulings of the highest court in our land? Who is he to be trying to humiliate America? Who is he to be dividing us? What is Cogan trying to do here? "The last time we saw Americans thinking that way," Fischer shouted, "it was called the Civil War."

The following afternoon, Mayor Partida got the call he'd been waiting for. His secretary had been instructed to put it right through no matter what he was doing.

"A Mr. Bruno is calling, Sir. He's on line three."

Partida hit the flashing button.

"Yes, Sir, Mr. Bruno. I've been expecting your call."

"How are you today, Mr. Mayor," Bruno inquired.

"Fine, just fine," Partida replied. "I understand you're going to be giving us some help on behalf of Mr. Ratson. I want to thank you for that."

"My pleasure. I'll be coming out sporadically myself, but in addition

I also wanted to make sure you had some experienced volunteers available. People who have handled delicate political projects and election issues before. So I'm sending out fourteen or fifteen people to assist in various tasks between now and November. They'll do things like voter registration, opposition research, press releases, survey work, and so on. They can report to a third party if you'd like—that way you can maintain deniability if anything goes wrong. We'll just have you sign a confidentiality agreement, and that will protect everybody. We like to be careful, you know, to avoid things like people writing books and such later on."

Partida was beside himself. Being asked to sign a confidentiality agreement with a big shot like Mr. Bruno! What next?

"Of course, of course," Partida said. "I'll be happy to sign. When can I expect the volunteers to arrive?"

"I hope it wasn't too presumptuous," Bruno said. "But they're already there."

Fischer picked up his phone on the second ring. Cogan was not usually a man to mince words, and he wasn't in the mood for making an exception.

"Hey, Mr. Missionary, you've been saying some pretty nasty things about me all over town."

"I think what you are doing is disgusting," responded Fischer.

"I don't give a damn what you think. But I do give a damn about what you're saying about me."

"If you can't stand the heat..."

"It's not about heat, it's about light. It's about the truth. Something you obviously don't care about," Cogan said.

"Well, I'll tell you what I do care about. I care about my country."

"If you cared about the things your country was founded to stand for, you'd be on the other side of this initiative from the one you're on."

"Cogan, you're a liar and a phony. You are using exaggerations and out-and-out deceit to paint America in a false, rotten light. You don't know what you're talking about. Your arguments don't stand the light of day, and you know it."

"Want to debate it?" Cogan shot back. "Or don't you have the balls?"

"Anytime, anywhere," Fischer replied.

"Fine," Cogan said, "You pick somebody to iron out the details on your behalf. Danielle Hall will take care of my side of it."

"She can deal with Paul Katz."

"Done. Be sure to tell all your Ivy League buddies to get there early and get good seats so they can watch you get your clock cleaned."

"Don't hold your breath."

Danielle and Katz set things up the next day. The debate would be held in four weeks, on October fourth, at the Fairview High School auditorium. The rules would be simple, but it would be no holds barred.

"This," Danielle reported to Cogan, "is going to be interesting." She immediately got on the phone and started alerting some of her key contacts in the media. Then she put together a short email. Within minutes the announcement went out to a small contingent of national media as well as local print and broadcast folks.

The meeting about the confidentiality statement had been scheduled on less than twenty-four-hours' notice. It took place in Partida's office and lasted less than five minutes. The lawyer—Wilfred somebody-or-other—barely introduced himself to Partida before pulling the contract out of his briefcase and placing it in front of the mayor. "This agreement," Wilfred frowned, "precludes you from revealing, discussing, or writing about anything that has transpired or transpires between yourself and Mr. Ratson, Mr. Bruno, and anyone working with them or on their behalf. You are agreeing not to disclose any of that to anyone at all. Do you have any questions?"

"No," Partida said, shaking his head.

"Good," Wilfred replied. "Please just sign and date the document, and I'll be on my way." As Partida signed, Wilfred mentioned that he would listen silently during any phone conversations between Partida and either Mr. Ratson or Mr.

Bruno. The reason for this was that so he could render legal advice to the parties. That seemed odd to Partida. Wilfred continued, explaining that the phone conversations, like the face-to-face ones, would all be attorney-client privileged. As a result, whatever was said would be completely confidential. It would be as though the conversations had never occurred. Period.

"Understood," Partida agreed. Boy, Wilfred was one serious guy. These D.C. folks knew how to cover their asses. They really didn't fool around. When Wilfred left Partida's office, he didn't even say goodbye.

CHAPTER NINETEEN

THE FORMER PRESIDENT

Ratson, a brilliant behind-the-scenes operator, had a reputation for being a master strategist. He had a photographic memory, an in-depth knowledge of politics, and the predatory instincts of a famished lion. With his national reputation and D.C. connections there was little he couldn't accomplish and even less he couldn't get away with. "Are you certain about this?" Ratson asked. The information he'd just been given was unbelievable. "If this turns out to be true, it will blow Cogan into the stratosphere. It will completely destroy his campaign."

"We haven't confirmed it yet," Bruno replied. "It's just a rumor we've picked up.

But we're going to check it out. We should know more in a matter of days."

Ratson smirked to himself. He understood how CenTel operated. He didn't know whether the rumors would turn out to be true, or not, and he didn't care one way or the other. As long as everybody had covered their asses. "A credible allegation about things like this," Ratson pointed out, "is all it would take to vaporize this whole initiative."

This was great. This was why Ratson had traded the courtroom for the back room in the first place. In a courtroom, everything was subject to rigorous analysis right in front of the judge and jury. What were you alleging? What was the basis for it? Who was making the assertion? Where was the proof? It was all about crossexamination and rigid rules. No hearsay, no argumentative questions, no irrelevance, no assumptions of facts not in evidence. You could attack testimony based on bias, prejudice, motive, perception. The witnesses were all under oath. It was hard to get away with anything. But politics was just the opposite. There were NO rules. Hearsay was just fine. Bias was part of the game. It was all about M and M: money and mudslinging.

"Whoever heard of a politician being sued for lying?" said Ratson. He and Bruno both got a chuckle out of that one.

"What would be the best way to get the information out there?" Bruno asked. "Press conference? Hit piece? The debate?"

Ratson thought about it for a few moments, tapping his fingers against the side of his face. Suddenly it came to him.

"I've got the answer," he said. "I'll handle it. Don't do anything further. Stay tuned."

Mayor Partida pounded his desk. Papers flew onto the floor, and pencils flipped up in the air. Partida had just learned, third hand, that a big debate over the initiative had been scheduled. Hundreds of voters would be there, maybe over a thousand—his constituents. The media would be out in force. Local, perhaps national, newspapers, TV and radio reporters. And he hadn't been invited to participate. Hell, he hadn't even been consulted about it. He was the mayor for Christ's sake. The goddamned mayor! And he had found out about it from one of his campaign volunteers. It was an outrage! That pompous son of a bitch Katz was undoubtedly behind it all.

"I'm not going to take this sitting down," Partida muttered as he dialed Ratson's private line.

He picked it up on the first ring. "Ratson here!" he barked. "Howie, it's James."

"How's it going, James?"

"I don't know, Howie," fretted Partida. "A debate's been scheduled between Cogan and this guy Mark Fischer."

"Who's Fischer?"

"Some guy that's been running all over town making, anti-initiative, anti-Cogan speeches. He's part of the Katz group."

"The speakers' bureau guy? Asked Ratson.

"Right."

"When's the debate?"

"In a few weeks," Partida replied. "And I wasn't even asked to take part. I have no familiarity at all with Fischer. I don't have any idea what the guy's going to say. But I'll bet the media's going to be there en masse."

"OK," Ratson said, "Just lay low. Don't say anything. Don't try to upstage anyone.

If reporters come up to you, tell them you'll have a statement after the debate. Then after it's all over, have a little press gathering outside or in a hallway. At that point, you can steal their thunder by making a strong, succinct, down-home statement. Say something like: 'Hey, I've been around public policy issues for a long time. I've got damn-good political instincts. And I'll tell you what. I don't trust this guy Cogan. Not one bit. I have a feeling that we haven't learned everything there is to know about Mr. Cogan. He's not the decent sort of man he's trying to portray. Mark my words. I'll stake my entire reputation on it. Then hold up a Fairview cap and wave it around and say: 'If I'm wrong about Cogan, I'll call a press conference and eat my hat on camera.'

"Do that and you'll be on every news clip that comes out of the debate."

Ratson was truly a genius. He deserved another cover story. "Shit," Partida said, "that's beautiful. Just beautiful. I'm sure glad you're on our side." He paused to scratch a mosquito bite on his right ankle. "But tell me, what do you have on Cogan that I should be willing to chance eating my hat over? On television, no less."

"Let your imagination run wild. Come up with a short list of the worst allegations you can think of that could be made against somebody in connection with an election campaign."

"It's that bad?"

"Worse," Ratson replied. "I don't want to discuss it on the phone, but it's huge. Don't breathe a word about any of this for now. Not to anyone. OK?"

"OK," Partida said as he hung up. But what in the world could it be?

Ironically, a few days before the debate, a $50,000 per person soft-money reception was being held for the Committee for American Values. The keynote speaker was a former president with strong ties to powerful business interests. The event was being held at the Four Seasons Hotel. With Danielle's best friend from high school serving as the special-events coordinator for the hotel, Sean got his hands on a caterer's uniform and simply showed up with little more than a goatee and some skin-darkening makeup as a disguise, Sean spent two hours serving stuffed hard-boiled eggs to a roomful of stuffed hard-boiled eggs. The appetizers were good, but the conversation was even better. With the press excluded and the riff-raff priced out, the guys really let their guards down.

Especially after a few drinks.

At last, the sound system kicked in, and the former leader of the free world walked in to the tune of Hail to the Chief. He was grinning like a frat rat, grabbing lucky hands, and pointing to people he pretended to know. In his short remarks, the former president joked about a pending attempt by Common Cause to place restrictions on events just like this one.

"What do you think about that idea?" he asked.

"BOOOOOOOOOOO" the audience responded. "BOOOOOOOOOOO."

"They should change their name to 'Common Corpse,'" the ex-pres smirked. "Their bill, which probably won't even make it out of committee, is already deader than Elvis." The congregation laughed. "They'd have a better chance of placing a windfall profits tax on CEO parachutes." More laughter. They were eating it up. "Or of nationalizing the oil industry."

"BOOOOOOOOOOOOO."

"Anyhoo, we'll win that battle. For you and for all Americans."

All multi-millionaire Americans, thought Cogan.

"So, I'll leave you with this. To paraphrase my old friends in the machine gun business, when big campaign contributions are outlawed; only outlaws will make big campaign contributions." The adoring crowd almost had a collective coronary on that one. "And so," the former president grinned, "I have a question. Do we have any outlaws in the room???"

"YEAAAHHHHHHHH" they bellowed.

"Now, I didn't ask that question, did I?"

"NOOOOOOOOOOOO," mooed the audience.

And with that, the XP, as he liked to call himself, took his leave and working the room as he walked, headed out to motorcade with five very special contributors en route to Buzzit—a plane named after its ability to run rings around Air Force One. He was headed out to Beverly Hills and then Newport Beach. Then on to Dallas and Palm Beach the next day. Then to Greenwich, Boston and finally the big one. Wall Street, with its latest batch of free marketeers floating high on their tax exemptions. He would avoid the demonstrators. That was never a problem. *So many rich folks*, thought XP as he floated across the room, *so little time*.

Sean headed back to the kitchen. Waiters were comparing tips. Bus boys and dishwashers were talking futbol scores; everybody was getting ready to go home to their spouses and kids. As he scrubbed off the makeup and removed his goatee for the drive back to Fairview, Cogan reflected on what he had just witnessed. It had been a remarkable experience, an incredible snapshot of the shot-callers. Just what he needed to psych himself up for what was surely about to come.

CHAPTER TWENTY

THE DEBATE

As the sun was casting an iridescent orange glow across the Fairview High School campus, the crowd began drifting in. Friends and neighbors joined strangers and reporters as camera crews and still photographers positioned themselves before the auditorium's stage. It was almost thirty minutes before the scheduled beginning of the debate and seats were already filled. The standing room crowd was spilling out into the hallway where speakers were being hastily set up to carry the proceedings to the SRO crowd.

Members of his office staff were holding places in the front row for Mayor Partida and his key NO-on-Prop A volunteers. Off to one side sat Jen, David, Geoffrey, Danielle, and Ollie. On the other side, Paul Katz chatted with the Fischer family and key members of the Katz opposition team. Scattered throughout the audience were Carl Sandgrow, the hardware store owner, realtor Wilma Nolan, town clerk Laurie Feinton, town attorney William Creswell, and his assistant, Jeb Holngren. In the shadows off on the right side, about halfway toward the rear, hunched the anonymous form of Bruno, whispering with his equally anonymous deputy, Mr. Cellphone, Joseph Iverson. Right behind them, looking every bit the part of a lost garage mechanic was Chris Mattington. On the left, sitting alone, was Sean's old friend, David Oster.

On stage, two empty folding chairs sat ten feet apart, separated by a stark podium. A facilities assistant stepped up to test the mike, tapping on it and repeating the magic words three times: "Testing, one two; testing, one, two; testing, one two." A hand signaled from the rear of the auditorium, indicating that the sound was okay. A few minutes passed as the din of conversation grew louder. Finally, the principal of Fairview High, a portly rumpled man in a wrinkled white dress shirt and ancient chinos, stepped up to the microphone.

"Welcome," he said, "I am Charles Hamilton, principal of Fairview High School, home of the famous Fairview Bulldogs." Scattered growling and barking sounds erupted among loyal Fairview High students and alums in the audience.

Unfortunately, these included Mayor Partida, who sounded more like a chihuahua than a bulldog. As cameras rolled, Hamilton, embarrassingly, barked back. For several uneasy moments, the principal and his students and former students made mad doggie sounds at each other while the rest of the audience stared at seat backs and window casements in near amazement, struggling to convince themselves that what they were hearing wasn't really happening.

"Enough," Principal Hamilton smiled, pleased that so many in the audience had demonstrated their continuing loyalty. "We are here in the best tradition of our democracy to witness a debate on Proposition A, which, as you know, will be on the ballot here in Fairview on this coming November 10. The proponents of Proposition A—known officially as the Fairview Self-Rule/Independence Initiative, will be represented tonight by its author, Sean Cogan. The opposition will be represented by Mark Fischer, who, I understand, has taken a leave of absence from his duties in Nairobi, Kenya in order to co-chair the NO-on-Prop A campaign. Mr. Cogan is a graduate of Stanford University. Mr. Fischer graduated from Brown. Both are grads of Fairview High." Scattered renewed yapping again broke out—this time somewhat less enthusiastically.

"Please welcome," Principal Hamilton said, "Sean Cogan and Mark

Fischer." Polite applause accompanied Cogan and Fischer as they walked onstage from opposite sides, nodded at each other apprehensively, and took their seats.

"By the rules previously agreed to, each side will make three presentations on whatever subjects relating to Proposition A it wishes. There are no holds barred and both can present or respond to whatever issues they would like. Each presentation is limited to fifteen minutes–a total an hour and a half in all. My role as moderator is simply to assure that the time limits are adhered to. "Mr. Fischer, by toss of the coin, we begin with you."

Mark Fischer stepped forward and started off by talking about his Nairobi project and how he was supposed to be in Africa working with Kenyan children rather than in Fairview fighting this initiative. He explained that he had come back to Fairview to celebrate his parents' thirty-fifth wedding anniversary and had intended to stay only a short time before returning to Nairobi. But when Paul Katz, a family friend, told him about Proposition A and asked him to stay and help in the effort to defeat it, he agreed. As important as his work was in Africa, where he tended to the sick and taught impoverished children to read and write, he became convinced that the NO-on-Prop A campaign was even more important.

"I've listened to some of Sean Cogan's speeches and interviews," he said, "and I must say, I am concerned. Many of us are worried about the increasing role that false assertions are playing in our politics. It's as though the wilder the conspiracy theories and outrageous allegations are, the more some people will believe them. And as we have seen, the consequences can be horrific. That is just what Sean is doing. Running around making crazy accusations left and right. He is trying to tell us that America's corporate officials and political institutions are corrupt, that our legislative process is in the pockets of special interests, that federal agencies are gratuitously spying on U.S. citizens, and that we are no longer a government of, by, and for the people. The facts behind some of these claims are totally exaggerated, and those behind others are completely false."

Fischer went on to argue that political campaigns, though expensive, were being financed by an increasingly broad base of support from large numbers of people who were putting their contributions were their mouths were. If people liked what their representatives were saying or doing, why shouldn't they be allowed to offer them financial support? Fischer cited statistics showing that over 80 percent of the contributors to congressional campaigns were individuals, not corporations.

Regarding claims by Cogan of payoffs for votes on legislation, Fischer argued that elected officials were subjected, as never before, to "scrutiny, oversight, analysis, and reanalysis by opponents, political commentators, consumer advocates, talk show pundits, bloggers, and, of course, lawyers." When serious wrongdoing is unearthed, he argued, people are drummed out of office as a result. "Publicity about these things," he said, "is not a sign of how bad our institutions are, but of how well the system is working."

Cogan sat there struggling to avoid reacting.

"And if you think some oil company executive can just write a fat campaign check to a U.S. senator one month and then watch him vote in favor of drilling for oil in Yosemite National Park two months later, you are dead wrong. Not only would such a senator be tarred and feathered all over the country, but he'd probably wake up with a subpoena on his pillow as well.

Regarding lobbyists, Fischer argued that anyone who knows how the system works understands that lobbyists perform extremely valuable services for the public at no charge to taxpayers. "A lot of legislation requires detailed knowledge in specialized areas. Topics from energy policy to specific military needs often requires a level of expertise that the average person simply doesn't have. Lobbyists provide that expertise.

"It is true," Fischer conceded, "that many lobbyists are on the payrolls of industry and corporate interests, and it is true that their job is to protect those interests from legislative grandstanding and abuse. But members of the House and Senate, and their staffs, are not idiots. They understand how to put what a lobbyist says in perspective. "In addition, there are strict rules that govern the activities of legislative advocates. Remember Jack Abramoff? Remember what happened to him? That's what happens when there are abuses.

"Next we have the topic of regulatory authorities. Mr. Cogan claims that government regulatory agencies are in the pockets of the interests they are supposed to be regulating. Give me a break, Sean. Tell that to the guy who wants to open a sandwich shop or start a wine distributorship. Businessmen and women can't spit without applying for three permits and four environmental impact reports. You need to hire a team of lawyers just to fire an employee who is pilfering petty cash. Not enough oversight? If we had any more oversight your kids would have to get a permit to have a lemonade stand in your driveway! Many in the audience were smiling and nodding. Fischer's points seemed to be hitting home.

"If you're a doctor willing to treat Medicare patients, you have to hire and pay a secretary just to handle all the paperwork. And that's nothing compared to what people go through in the oil, insurance, banking, food processing, building supply, importing, exporting, toy manufacturing, construction, and most other businesses. Regulators in the pockets of industry? HA."

"Time is up, Mr. Fischer," interrupted Principal Hamilton, "it's Mr. Cogan's turn."

Fischer sat down to a warm round of applause as Sean Cogan rose to speak.

"I want to express my admiration for the work Mark Fischer is doing in Kenya. He deserves our respect for that." The audience applauded politely. "But Mr. Fischer sees our government very differently than I do—in a number of important ways.

First, there is one thing we agree on. The impact that false conspiracy theories and exaggerated allegations have on our society are devastating.

They completely undermine our confidence and our ability to govern ourselves. That is not what I am doing or have done. To the contrary, every single charge that I am leveling at our governmental and financial institutions is one-hundred per cent accurate. And I challenge you, Mr. Fischer to cite a single example to the contrary.

"Let's talk about political campaigns. In order to have a government of, by, and for the people, you have to have representatives you can access.

Representatives who are going to listen to you and promote policies based on your interests. Let me ask you. Show me by raising your hands. How many of you think you could get through personally to your congressional representative about pending or proposed legislation if you called in to his office?"

Not a hand went up.

"Want to have a little fun? Call your congressman on Monday and try to get through in your own name. Then wait half an hour and call using the name of any of the people listed as having attended his last big-ticket fundraiser. If your guy is in the office, guess what's going to happen?" Nervous laughter was spreading quickly.

"How many of you have ever contributed $10,000 or more to your congressional representative?"

No hands.

"Or to a PAC? A Political Action Committee?"

No hands.

"OK. Let's forget about $10,000. Let's try $50,000? $100,000?

"Why do you think the oil industry, big banks, agribusiness, insurance companies, pharmaceutical companies, et cetera contributed ten times that amount—and more—to congressional fundraisers, alone, last year.

"Eighty percent of the total number of *contributors* may be individuals not corporations, but ninety percent of the money 'contributed' comes from billionaires and corporations.

"And lobbyists. Mr. Fischer paints them as OUR little helpers saving us money by helping write our laws. How many of you think AIG's lobbyists are OUR little helpers? Or Merrill Lynch's? Or Bank of America's? Or Chevron's? Or Blue Cross's? Or Bechtel's? Or Pfizer's? Or GE's? Or Mass Mutual's? Or Monsanto's?

"Turning to corporate corruption. Mr. Fischer would have you believe that I am exaggerating the problem. On the contrary, if anything, I am understating it. What I am talking about is only a fraction of the problem. I am referring to everything from the bribing of foreign and domestic government officials in exchange for the awarding of contracts to the fact that the senior executives of some of the largest banks in the country have bilked employee pension funds. How about the way that corporate execs pay off third-world potentates to allow the illegal shipping of carcinogenic waste material to be sent illegally to toxic chemical dumps in their countries?" Cogan went on to detail dozens of corporate scandals that filled headlines over that year alone. "And those are the ones we know about. Those are the guys that were caught!

"Excessive regulation. Mr. Fischer talks about excessive regulations imposed on sandwich shop owners and food distributors and doctors. He warns about our kids having to get a permit to set up a lemonade stand. But what about the big guys? What about how the elimination of banking and securities regulations brought us to the brink of a global depression? What about the seniors who lost their retirement savings? Or the over 25 percent of college graduates who can't find jobs but are being harassed to pay back their student loans? Or the predatory lending schemes by all of the big banks that forced hundreds of thousands of people into foreclosure and bankruptcy? All of this going on while CEOs were getting multimillion dollar golden parachutes whether their companies and stockholders are doing well or suffering huge financial losses!

"Why is all of this happening? Just look to who's paying the piper. And here's a clue, Mr. Fischer. It's not the kids with their lemonade stand.

"Let's move on to personal freedom. Freedom of speech. The right to privacy. Freedom of the press. Freedom of association. Over two hundred years ago these rights were written into the Constitution by the Founding

Fathers for the specific purpose of protecting future generations not from foreign enemies but from their own government. These are not just American rights; they are human rights.

"Yet just look at some of the things that have become commonplace events in our country.

"Freedom of speech? On the pretext of quelling disturbances the National Guard will often combine with local Tac Squads to beat demonstrators protesting things like international economic conferences, U.S. foreign policy, global warming, or the ten-thousand-square-mile garbage dump that is sitting in the middle of the Pacific Ocean.

"Privacy? The NSA uses data mining to compile logs on virtually all telephone calls in the U.S. from American Internet companies. Microsoft, Google, Apple, Yahoo, Skype are tapping into hundreds of high capacity fiber optic cables monitoring over four hundred lines at once. The NSA also compiles medical records, financial information, and God knows what else on all of us.

"Freedom of the press? Under the guise of exercising their enforcement authority, reporters are arrested and thrown in jail for refusing to turn over the names of confidential whistle blowers who had provided proof of illegal activities by government agencies.

"Freedom of association? Time and time again, government agents routinely intimidate citizens by photographing and tape recording them at the scene of lawful protests." It was Fischer's turn to roll his eyes in disbelief.

Cogan went on about other issues having to do with everything from the insulation of insurance companies from liability for bankrupting claimants by defrauding them out of medical and disability benefits to immunizing the Army Corps of Engineers against liability for incompetently designed flood-control projects.

"I could go on," Cogan said, glancing at his watch, "but I'm running overtime. So I'll just leave it at this. The one thing Mr. Fischer and I agree on is that this is no ordinary election, and Proposition A is no ordinary ballot initiative. We are a people in crisis. A crisis that no single person can solve. If we, here in our little town of Fairview, don't join forces and say enough, that we are reclaiming our God-given human rights now, then we will have no one to blame for the consequences but ourselves."

The audience response to Cogan was also strong. People hooted and shouted as

Jen shot him a big smile. When the applause died down, Principal Hamilton spoke.

"Mr. Fischer, it's your turn."

Fischer took a deep breath. "If I believed half of what Mr. Cogan just said," he deadpanned, "I'd be packing up and moving to Canada. But I don't. I don't buy it. His allegations are so filled with distortions, lies, and half-truths that it's hard to know where to begin. Let's take some of these things one at a time.

"Data mining? Why should I be concerned about who knows who I telephone? Financial transactions? They're in every credit report. Medical records? Insurance companies have them all anyway. Asset information? It's on every loan application. Computer records? Go Google yourself. It's all there —without any government involvement. The bottom line for all of this is who cares? People who don't have anything to hide are not whining about their inability to hide it.

"And here's the point: If we are going to stop terrorists, if we are going to halt their schemes before they can carry them out, we have to use every means at our disposal. Infiltration, wire-tapping, surveillance, computer data collection— everything. We have to be smarter, faster, and more thorough than they are. We can't be sitting around applying for search warrants or filing motions in courts asking for permission to listen in on them. Let's get real here. Our government is after the enemy. We have to let it do the job.

Fischer went on to explain his take on the global issues involving the shrinking world economy. He seemed to be getting a mixed reception on this, but people were listening. He moved on to the subject of executive compensation.

"Regarding," he said, "the so-called golden parachutes problem we have all heard about. For Mr. Cogan to be using this to create a poster child for demonizing our governmental and corporate systems is really a cheap shot. The bottom line is that how much a company negotiates to pay its own senior management should really be up to it. A good CEO is a valuable asset whose daily decisions can put hundreds of millions of dollars in the pockets of shareholders." Fischer seemed to catch himself as audience members started to snicker at the suggestion that some of these managers had done anything good for their companies at all.

"Here's the bottom line," he stumbled. "We live in a diverse nation and in controversial times. But if you don't like things that are going on, that doesn't mean you should try and pull out. When union members were beaten for organizing, they didn't talk about doing that. When women couldn't vote they didn't talk about doing that. When blacks couldn't go to white schools, they didn't talk about doing that. There are always going to be flaws in any system. There will always be things you can point to that seem unfair and even absurd. But you don't respond by trying to pull out. Mr. Cogan is trying to use a chain saw to perform microsurgery.

"So, my question is why are you doing this, Sean? Why do you want to throw the baby out with the diaper? Why jump off a cliff?" Fischer looked down at Cogan, grinning. "Lighten up, man!"

The crowd chuckled at that one. Fischer's parents found it particularly hilarious, laughing and snorting loudly.

Principal Hamilton turned to Cogan. "You're up, Mr. Cogan.

"I apologize, Mr. Fischer," Cogan said, with a flash of anger, "if it seems like I'm taking this too seriously, if it seems like I should lighten up." He turned to the audience. "But to me this is a very serious situation. My response to Mr. Fischer is going to be brief.

"Listen. Listen to what Mr. Fischer has said today. Because that is what he believes. On multimillion-dollar campaign contributions? They are like you and me giving a hundred bucks to a congressperson we like.

On data mining? Who cares? On the destruction of the freedoms granted by our Bill of Rights? He doesn't believe it. On lobbyists writing our laws? They're only helping. On golden parachutes? It's up to the individual corporations.

"My beliefs are the exact opposite of Mr. Fischer's on all of these issues. And frankly, I don't understand how he can say any of those things. Didn't all of us here over the age of thirty grow up believing that we had a right to live in a land of the free? Where a person could believe and think and stand for and do and be what he pleased. Where we the people ruled the government rather than the other way around. Where you could hang out with whomever you wanted and could say whatever you felt like saying without fear that some nosy bureaucrat in a starched shirt and pressed jeans would be listening in and writing reports about it. Didn't we all grow up understanding that bribes and payoffs—by whatever name or rationale—were bad and that people, not vested interests, were supposed to be the focal point of our society?"

Cogan talked about other things. The arrogance of the IRS. The cold-heartedness of the Veterans Administration. The audacity of the Social Security

Administration. The general unresponsiveness of all government agencies with their voice mail, their endless menu choices, and Muzak driving you crazy when you're on hold. He went on for a bit about the latter, launching into a semi-diatribe about Leslie Gore crying if she wanted to. At that point the crowd began snickering and laughing, perhaps in agreement, perhaps not

Hamilton suddenly cut in. "OK," he said. "Time is up Mr. Cogan. Your turn, Mr. Fischer. This is the third and final round." Fischer paused, struggling to conceal his surprise at the crowd's reaction to Cogan. He had wanted to avoid going on the attack—going negative—but he felt he had to turn the audience against Cogan.

"All right," he said, looking down on his opponent and addressing him directly. "Enough is enough. I'm sorry, but I just have to say this.

You are trying to come off as some kind of high-minded, good-humored person. But you are no such thing. High-minded, good-humored people do not betray our country. They do not knowingly accuse their nation's leaders of criminal misconduct. Of hypocrisy. Of violating their oaths of office. Such accusations are hard to characterize without resorting to strong language. The word 'treasonous' comes to mind."

You could feel the reaction. A collective hush came over the audience. Fischer tried to recover. "Treason is a strong word, but what else would you call it when someone sets out to get people to turn against their country?"

Cogan could feel the hair tingling on the back of his neck. The muscles in his face started to twitch. His ears grew red hot.

"Look," Fischer said, "I'm not saying America is perfect, but it's the best system I know of, anywhere. And the idea of asking people to throw in the towel is, to me, unfathomable.

"If Mr. Cogan really wanted to bring about change in Washington, he would simply go out and register voters who share his points of view. We have congressional elections coming up in just a little over a year. If enough people agree with him, they can just vote the people they don't like out of office." The man on the left in front of Mattington cast a disgusted look toward the man to his right. "This is what I was afraid of." He scowled. "Ratson is not going to be happy when he hears Fischer is playing up this argument. If the media pick up on it, it could present a problem. Campaigns sprouting up all over the place to turn the rascals out. This is exactly why McMann wants to bury Cogan now and not be screwing around."

Mattington was shocked. His inconspicuous presence, excellent hearing, and new Radio Shack sound amplifier might well be leading the way to a great story. Who were these two, he wondered? Ratson? Was it possible that they were talking about Howard Ratson? THE Howard Ratson? If so, some of the most powerful figures in Washington had to be involved in this as well. Right up to their eyelashes. Mattington smiled to himself as he cranked up the volume and aimed his new device at the two strangers sitting in front of him.

"... Register voters," repeated Fischer, "and raise the issues you care about. Elect new leaders, new members of the House and Senate—if you think that's necessary. But I'll tell you something—don't complain if reform elections don't give you the results you want. People from South Carolina don't have the right to choose our representatives, and we don't have the right to choose theirs. We all have the right to elect whomever we want. That's our system. And it has worked very well for the past 200 plus years.

Fischer paused for a good ten seconds to let his points sink in. Finally, he continued. "And so, I'll close by simply saying thank you for coming to this debate tonight and thank you for having paid such close attention, I ask you to continue to pay close attention in the closing days prior to the election. I ask you to continue to believe in the things that our country has always stood for, and that the United States—the *United States*—stands for today.

"On behalf of the NO-on-Proposition A campaign, I ask each and every one of you to help us between now and November 10 in our get-out-the-vote efforts and to give us your vote on election day.

"Vote NO. NO on divisiveness. NO on lies. NO on exaggeration. NO on proposition

A. Thank you." The audience responded strongly. Some stood and applauded.

"Your final statement, Mr. Cogan," Principal Hamilton said.

Danielle held her breath. She caught Cogan's eye just long enough to say, "Keep it calm, Sean. Hold your temper..."

"I won't even comment on Mr. Fischer's name calling" he said. Jen and Danielle breathed a heavy sigh of relief. "Except to say that I am surprised he would stoop to such tactics. Frankly, I thought more of him than that.

"Responding to the issue of voting out corrupt incumbents and reforming corporate lawlessness, I wish I could say—I wish I could believe—that we could just do that. But we cannot.

"There's a book by Mark Weston, a public interest lawyer from New York City, called *Highest Bidder*. The book lays out the whole problem involving the correlation between money and politics. *Highest Bidder* lays out statistically all of the proof needed to show why reform efforts have not and cannot work. Suffice it to say that with only extremely rare exceptions, there is a direct relationship between how much money a candidate spends and how many votes he or she receives. It really is all about money. And because in congressional races, the big money all comes from special interests, those interests will always control the system. That's the way special interests want it, and that's the way it is. We are powerless to change it and powerless to stop it.

"It's not about people from one congressional district electing someone the people from another district don't like. It's about people from every congressional district being manipulated by multi-million dollar campaigns funded by billionaire special interests. It's about having the best politicians money can buy—in every congressional district. It's about the fact that our representatives have, purely and simply, legalized payoffs.

"I touched," Cogan went on, "only in passing on the issue of federal judges. But that is a very big issue. There are, today, thousands of extremely pro-big business federal trial and appellate judges in place. These judges have all been appointed with the calculated approval of special interests. All of them have permanent appointments. All of them will remain in power for the rest of their lives. They are positioned to issue rulings and make decisions that will take us through the next thirty years. And there's hardly an anti-big business judge among them. I can assure you that if there's anything big money can't accomplish through payoffs, TV ads, and political campaigns, it will achieve through court rulings.

"I haven't had time to talk about our tax system, in which ordinary people pay a higher percentage of their income in taxes than do the big oil, banking, manufacturing, pharmaceutical and insurance companies—many of whom, on billions in profits, pay no U.S. taxes at all. That contributes to the incredible, absurd, outrageous truth that the top one tenth of one percent of our citizens own as much wealth as the entire bottom ninety percent.

"We have a child poverty rate that is twice as high as countries like Germany, Poland, Korea, Australia, and the Czech Republic. And while 32.2% of our children are living in poverty, the presidents and CEOs of major U S corporations are making ten and twenty and thirty million dollars per year and more. A government of, by and for the people? Which people?

"I haven't had time to talk about our nation's spending priorities, in which we manage to find hundreds of billions of dollars for rearming nuclear missiles capable of destroying the entire planet seven times over but can't find the revenue needed to adequately subsidize schools or college tuition payments or veterans benefits for people who have had arms and legs blown off in our foreign wars.

"The bottom line, the sad truth, is that big money is not GOING to win; it has ALREADY won. And we have no other choice than to either capitulate to this or to reject it.

"And I say that if we want to get our freedom back, we have to throw down the gauntlet. To vote for our independence and to vote for our freedom. To vote for a government that once again is accountable to us."

Pausing to collect his thoughts, he continued. "There have been some disagreements here tonight with regard to what the government is doing, to whom, and why. With respect to these disagreements I am also going to ask you for a commitment. I am going to ask you to pay very close attention to what transpires between now and November 10. To matters that I believe will be surfacing between now and then.

"I especially ask you to watch the Connolly Show this coming Tuesday. I will be Mr. Connolly's guest, and given this issue, and Mr. Connolly's temperament and political philosophy, it promises to be interesting.

"And on November 10, I urge you to vote: Yes for freedom. Yes for independence. Yes for standing up to billion dollar special interests. Yes to limits on campaign contributions. Yes on Fairview steering its own course. Yes to an end of tolerating graft and corruption. Yes on Proposition A.

"Like Mr. Fischer, I thank you for coming this evening and for being so attentive. Good Night."

The audience's nervous, somewhat tentative, applause continued as the media descended on both speakers. As the departing crowd mingled after the debate, Mattington, pretending to be listening to his voice mail, had shuffled near the strangers he had been sitting behind, trying to pick up any additional information he could. At one point the larger of the two men referred to the shorter one as Iverson. He also picked up a name they were talking about. Somebody called McCann or McMann. It sounded as though they were talking about some kind of investigator. Using his cellphone, Mattington inconspicuously snapped a digital photo of the two as they stood, preoccupied with their discussion. A few minutes later he tried to strike up a conversation. "What did you think of the debate?" he asked them. His attempt got nowhere. Neither of them had any interest in chatting with a stranger.

"Interesting," the taller one mumbled, turning back to his friend. Minutes later, as the crowd started easing out toward the parking lot, Mattington watched as they got into a new Toyota Celica. License plate R920 EBG. It turned out to be owned by a local Hertz affiliate. It had been rented the day before to an Alfonse Bruno of Houston, Texas. Within hours Mattington had obtained Bruno's driver's license number, his home and cell telephone numbers, and his Visa number.

Mayor Partida pointed to the door, signaling to a television crew and several reporters that he would be waiting outside. Fifteen minutes later, after they were done taking sound bites from local residents, corralling them for their conclusions, and quizzing them about how they expected to vote, the press descended on Principal Hamilton to ask about the source of the doggie cheer. They then wandered outside to find Partida waiting with a few staffers by a tall Sycamore tree. Emboldened by the refreshment he had downed from his thermos to ward off the evening chill, he did exactly as he had been coached.

"Sean Cogan is not to be trusted," Partida slurred, "Not at all. And I predict that you will see this. You will see it as the coming days come to pass.

"And I am so sure I am right, so very sure," he declared, waiving his Bulldogs hat in the air for the cameras, "that if I am wrong, I will eat my hat—in public, on the steps of town hall." The reporters loved it. They would, they promised, follow up. One way or the other.

They all gathered back at Jen's house to celebrate and plan the closing weeks of the campaign. Geoffrey would be organizing the YES on Prop A campaigns getout-the- vote effort. Danielle would be monitoring the media coverage of the debate, and preparing for the Connolly Show. Ollie would be having some last minute meetings with his supporters. Everyone had jobs to do.

Slowly, the group dissipated, leaving Cogan and Jen alone, at last. Cogan looked sullen. "Fischer got me with the traitor business, didn't he," he said. "I could see it in their faces. That got a reaction. It scared them."

"Come here, big guy," Jen laughed, pulling him into her arms "You're no traitor, and anyone with the slightest amount of common sense knows that. Don't worry about it. You did a kick ass job."

Cogan hoped Jen was right. "Maybe," he said. "We'll see. It probably depends on what happens between now and election day." Jen didn't know what Cogan was talking about. She would soon be finding out.

CHAPTER TWENTY-ONE

THE HONORABLE VAUGHN SAWTON

The Honorable Vaughn Sawton, chair of the Senate Appropriations and Armed Services Committees, founder of the American Business Coalition (ABC), and one of the most prolific fundraisers in the country, was a very powerful man. His staff nicknamed him Chainsaw, and only they knew whether that was a play on his last name, an inside joke about his personality, or both.

Sawton, a Democrat, had arrived in the nation's capital, twenty years before Fairview's ballot proposition, with barely enough money to keep his checking account active. By the time Cogan and Fischer debated, he was one of the wealthiest men in Congress. Chainsaw's office was in the Russell Senate Office building, a structure constructed from 1903 to 1905 and named in 1972 for white supremacist Georgia Senator Richard Russell, the coauthor of the anti-civil rights Southern Manifesto. Sawton had no problem with that. The building was ironically located on Constitution Avenue in Northeast Washington.

It was 10:10, five minutes before David Henninger and Howard Ratson were scheduled to meet with Senator Sawton. They knew from experience that they'd be ushered into his office at precisely 10:14. Even with friends and close associates, Chainsaw ran his schedule with a Swiss hourglass. At 10:12, by Henninger's watch, Sawton's deputy chief of staff entered the anteroom to usher them inside. That could mean only one thing, Henninger decided: his watch was two minutes off. They were greeted with the stiff, icy grin for which Chainsaw was famous.

"Howie, how're the kids? How's Theresa?" Before Ratson could answer,

Chainsaw was on to David. "David, say hello to Maureen for me. How's she doing? How did her back surgery go?"

"Very well, Sir, thank you for asking. How's your family? How is your daughter enjoying Cornell?"

"Great, thanks. Just great. So, cutting to the meat of it, Howie, I read your memo. Very good. Very helpful. The part about how you're going to get the word out is pure genius. Let me know the date. Of course as soon as I finished reading it, I shredded it. You should do likewise. No copies. No email trail. Take care of it if you haven't already."

"Already have, Sir."

"Always a step ahead. Good."

"What are your thoughts on the matter, Senator?"

"Well," Chainsaw said, "first, let me tell you that I've asked one of my lawyers, Richard—over there in the corner—to sit in for this discussion, so everything here is privileged and never happened. You don't have to worry, Richard's a great guy and all, sharp as cut glass, but he can't hear a damn thing. He's as deaf as driftwood." As he spoke, Chainsaw smiled his stiff grin and nodded toward Richard, who was paging through a magazine.

"Ok, here's the deal," he said. "Bob Vissel over at the FBI will rubber stamp whatever needs to be done. OK? So, you've got your cover through the Bureau. But you're in charge. You decide whatever. And I'm not involved with anything. I don't need to be. Shit, even now, I can't recall whether we met or what we talked about."

"Right," Ratson said.

"We're with you, Sir," Henninger agreed.

"Ok. Fine. So that's it. It's done. David, what's happening outside of this? Is Bama going to beat Clemson this year? Chop 'em up and ship 'em out again?"

"Lookin' good, Sir."

Chainsaw glanced down at his watch. "Gotta go." He laughed. "Meeting with the Sultan of someplace or other. Taylor will give me his name before he slithers in here. The guy farts petro dollars. He wants the Senate to keep its nose out of his role in the price-fixing fiasco. Ha! Fine. But it will cost him. It'll cost him big time. Shit. What a job this is. Thank God for the Caribbean, eh? Bye, boys," Chainsaw said, standing. "See ya' soon. Good hunting."

Just like that, with a nod and a little wave of his stubby fingers, the meeting was over. As they left, Henninger wondered why they didn't pass any sultans in the anteroom. Then he remembered. There were two anterooms.

Once they were back outside, walking down toward the Capital Mall, Ratson turned to Henninger. "What was that 'Thank God for the Caribbean' business? What was that about?"

"Hold on for a second," Henninger replied, making small talk until they were some distance away. Finally, he spoke. Practically beneath his breath, "The Caribbean," he said. "Numbered bank accounts. Just a few hours away."

CHAPTER TWENTY-TWO

THE CONNOLLY SHOW

Cogan sat on the black leatherette chair before a bank of lights. Sadie, who had bright red hair and stood five-foot-three on her toes, was Billy Bob Connolly's makeup artist in chief. She was doing her best to make Cogan look presentable, but the stuff she was applying made his face feel dry and crackly. "What are you here to joust with the boss about?" she asked.

"About why I'm so fed up that I put an initiative on the ballot in Fairview calling for the town to declare its independence from the Union."

"Oh, are you that guy?" Sadie asked.

"Yep."

"I've heard all about you." She grinned.

Cogan sat there waiting for Sadie to respond by smearing his face with something indelible five minutes before airtime. At the very least, he expected a warm-up God-Bless-America rant coupled with a broadside challenging his loyalty, patriotism, and judgment. It didn't happen.

"Whoooop-dee-doo," Sadie howled. "Great! When you're done out there, you should come back here and run the same campaign in Brooklyn!"

"Wait a second. You work for Connolly. How..."

"Hey," Sadie interrupted, "those light bulbs you're staring into are a hell of a lot brighter than Billy Bob."

"You don't like him, I guess."

"Nobody likes him. I'm told that his own mother denies she's related to him. Ever been on the show before?" she asked. "No, I haven't," Cogan replied, "why?"

"Let me give you a few tips. Smile a lot. Don't let him put words in your mouth. Listen for a while without interrupting. Let him go on and on. Then, have your pitch ready. Short and sweet. Stick to your points. Don't get into one of those interrupting battles with him. He will try and bait you every way he can. He's really good at provoking people in a way that makes them look bad. Stay cool. The calmer you are, the more frustrated he'll get.

"The one thing he can't stand is to be laughed at or joked about. That really makes him bounce off the walls. So if he starts to lose control, just smile and say something like: 'Oh, Connolly, you're such a lunatic.' Then laugh at him. He will go totally nuts.

"OK," Sadie said, stepping back and admiring her work. "Beautiful. Perfect. You're done. Go get him."

"I'm ready for the dance?"

"Yep."

"Thanks," Cogan replied.

"I'll be watching on the monitor," Sadie grinned.

"Mr. Cogan?" came the voice as the door popped open. "Are you set?"

"I am."

"Ok. Let's go."

Cogan was led down the hall and into the studio. There were four cameras set at varying angles, all aimed at the familiar, blotchy face sitting in the middle of the room. Technicians wearing headphones whispered orders into their microphones. Ushered to a stiff backless chair that felt as uncomfortable as it looked, Cogan glanced at Connolly, expecting a nod or handshake. All he got was a glare. Apparently Billy Bob—who liked to be called Mr. Right—was trying to psych him out just before going on the air.

"Thirty seconds," shouted one of the headphones guys.

Connolly sat up, moistened his lips, straightened his tie, cleared his throat, stretched his neck, and tugged back on the tail of his jacket.

"Five... four... three... two..." point, background music, "GO."

"Good evening," Connolly said. "And welcome to the Connolly Show. This evening we have what I would call an unusual guest—even by our outside-the-box standards. Mr. Sean Cogan, a retired millionaire."

Okay, thought Cogan, *Here he goes...*

"Mr. Cogan," growled Connolly, "in what would seem a bizarre and desperate move to draw attention to himself and to embarrass his country, has put an initiative together, to have local voters—get this— DECLARE THEIR

INDEPENDENCE. And he wants the town to be able to ignore any laws or court decisions that it disagrees with. Is that right, Sean?"

"Well, actually..."

"Wait a second. Wait a second, is what I just said correct, or incorrect? Let's at least start this off by just agreeing to the given. OK? You want Fairview to slip out the back Jack, isn't that right? You want to abandon the USA. In the middle of terrorist attacks on Americans, with beheadings, torture, bombings, war and all the rest, you want Americans in Fairview to quit. Basically to vote to bail out, correct?"

"What I am trying to..."

"C'mon, Sean," he pressed, turning to glare at him dead-on, "answer the question."

Jen sat in the waiting area watching the monitor.

"So. Mr. Cogan," Connolly scowled, "you are a citizen righteously outraged. Your sense of morality and decency have been offended by what you consider to be the many transgressions of the governmental and corporate institutions of this country. Our leadership in America has trampled upon your rights as an ordinary citizen. You believe you have been abused by our government. You feel ignored by the system.

Correct?"

"Yes."

"By the House and Senate? Correct?"

"Yes."

"You feel betrayed by our country's foreign policies. Correct?"

"Yes."

"And by its domestic policies. Correct?"

"Yes."

"And by appointments that have been made in recent years to the federal district and appellate courts. Correct?"

"Yes."

Cogan started to squirm a bit. His chair was extremely uncomfortable. He guessed that was intentional. He was right.

"And by our budget priorities. Correct?"

"Yes."

"You feel that we're spending too much money on guns and not enough on butter. Correct?"

"Yes."

"You believe that politicians are being paid off by the special interests. Correct?"

"Yes."

"You believe that corporations are awash in corruption. Correct?"

"Yes."

"You believe the government is invading our privacy. Correct?"

"Yes."

"And is abridging freedom of speech, freedom of the press, freedom to assemble, and other constitutional freedoms. Correct?"

"Yes." The lights seemed to be getting hotter by the second.

"That the House and Senate have passed legislation giving the green light to all those presumed transgressions."

"Yes."

"You are outraged with government agencies, the income tax system, and telephone access.

"Well... "

"You don't think anything can be done about any of these things from within the system because you have concluded that there's no way to beat big money at its game. Correct?"

"Yes."

"You no longer consider the United States to be the land of the free. Correct?"

"Yes."

"The tiny town of Fairview is going to be your new land of the free. With, among other things, your own laws, your own law enforcement system, your own judges, your own constitution, your own priorities, everything. Correct?"

"Yes."

"See there." Connolly smiled, "I've done my homework on what you stand for, haven't I?"

"Seems like it," replied Cogan.

"Well, guess what, Mr. Cogan," frowned Connolly, "I've also done my homework on you—on you, personally. And I don't think you're going to like what I've found out. I don't think you're going to like it one little bit. More," Connolly said, "after this brief word from our sponsors."

Following one commercial featuring an insurance company promising always to be there in times of need and another pitching iron supplements for seniors, the cameras came back on.

"One of the main things you are going after our government for is alleged spying on innocent citizens, correct?"

"I have said that many of the practices that have been perpetrated by the government are terrifying. That if you go back and look at the four-hundred-page Patriot Act enacted back in 2001, at the Defense Authorization Act of 2006, at the communications immunity provisions of 2008, at the amendments to that bill that were subsequently enacted, as recently as last year, you will see that Congress has expressly authorized domestic spying, established a national police force, created secret prisons, authorized the government to use torture in interrogating prisoners, and on and on."

"Why don't you just tell our viewers all about how you stand to benefit personally if Fairview is able to rewrite our laws, set up its own government, establish its own judicial system, and bar police authorities from obtaining evidence in criminal cases from peoples' computers and telephone records."

"What do you mean," Cogan asked, "by benefit personally?"

"You tell us, Mr. Cogan. Tell us what you do in your spare time as a retired multimillionaire. Tell our viewers about the drugs and about the child pornography that you are involved with."

Sweat was pouring from Cogan's forehead. Connolly, he thought, must put heat lamps over his guests' chairs. The host was practically laughing at this point. He was really going to nail Cogan's ass. Another free spirit would soon be eating elephant dung on national television. On his show.

In the makeup room, Sadie's mouth dropped open. Across the country, people gasped. In Fairview restaurants, bars, and homes, residents were shocked. Incredulous. Although it was true that Connolly was a nut, he would never make such an allegation on national television in front of millions of people if he couldn't prove it. If this wasn't true, Connolly would not only be ruining his own reputation, he would be costing his network millions.

It must be true! How could Sean Cogan have done that? How could he have convinced his closest friends and supporters that he was such a good and decent guy, that he was so sincere, if all along he was a horrible, terrible person?

Connolly continued. "You are the one who is leading this charge," he pressed. "You are Fairview's answer to George Washington. C'mon Sean, I'm sure you cannot tell a lie. Don't be shy. The truth of the matter is that the government you hate so much has been conducting a year-long investigation of you involving child pornography and drug dealing. In fact, you knew you were going to be indicted. And so you came up with the scheme of this ballot initiative so you could profess your innocence and claim you were being set up because of your political activities. Isn't that so?"

Connolly didn't know what to expect from Cogan in response. A torrent of indignation, a challenge to Connolly's sources, a tearful denial, or something he couldn't guess.

Cogan stayed cool. He was prepared for the attack. "Two minutes, Mr. Connolly, I would like an uninterrupted two minutes to respond to your horrible, false, allegations. Fair enough?"

Connolly really had no choice. "Go ahead. Be my guest," he snickered.

Cogan put his briefcase on his lap and pulled out a sheaf of papers before Connolly could object. He held some papers up to the camera. "Here are photographs of men breaking into my house and..."

Forgetting his two-minute commitment, Connolly interrupted. "Just a second, just a second." Connolly was a pro. He didn't miss a beat. "Men breaking into your house. Blurred photographs taken from behind. Men with no faces! And you just happened to be sitting there with a camera when those guys broke in. How stupid do you think my audience is? You are full of it, Cogan. You knew you were going to be charged, and you set up these phony photographs, ones taken from the rear. Probably with your criminal cohorts."

Cogan exploded. "Connolly, you lying son of a bitch."

"That's it," Connolly sputtered, "no one is going to come on my show and insult my audience with obscenities. No one. Much less a manipulative, drug-dealing, child-porn-peddling traitor. Get out. Get off my set, or I'll throw you off. We're going to break for a commercial, and when we come back you are going to be gone." Connolly turned to his camera. "I apologize," he said to his audience, "for insulting your intelligence with the likes of Mr. Cogan. When we return, I promise—one way or the other—he won't be here."

Suddenly, Cogan looked like he'd been sucker punched. As soon as they were off camera, two security guards walked up to Cogan, poised to remove him from the set if he didn't leave on his own. As he departed, he turned and shouted to Connolly: "Who gave this to you, you bastard? Who?" Connolly's only answer was to smile.

When their plane landed, Sean and Jen drove straight to Sean's house. Logging on to his computer, his IM box immediately popped up from his favorite religious nut. It was inconceivable that Moe-zus didn't watch Connolly. "Hey Pal," he began, "I should have known. A lefty, a druggie, and a child porno king all rolled up into one big disloyal ball of filth. Tell me, how do you live with your disgusting self?"

"Don't believe everything you are told by sanctimonious, right-wing, kooky, creationists. They will try and ply you with whatever raw meat they can get their fat little hands on."

"I'll bet you anything you want that you'll never slither out of this one," Moe-zus wrote.

"You're on," Cogan replied.

"What are we betting?"

"If you eventually conclude I'm not guilty of any of the things Connolly accused me of, you donate a hundred dollars to Planned Parenthood—in the name of Moe-zus."

"And if I don't?"

"Then I'll give the hundred to the church of your choice."

"We've got a deal."

"Ok," Cogan said, "keep your checkbook handy.

"Ha, pervert," responded Moe-zus, "you gonna need a miracle."

An hour later, two uniformed deputies arrived at the Cogan home. Cogan counted half a dozen photographers and six news cameras. They had been camping out for hours, just in case, and they were there, waiting, when the patrol car arrived. Cogan smiled as he answered the front door wearing jogging shorts and a t-shirt proclaiming YES ON PROP A. He smiled and waved to the reporters and invited the officers inside. It struck Cogan as incredible that he was still managing to get through everything that was happening to him. Some of the same people who four months before had thought of him as a well-to-do retired money manager and part-time venture capitalist now saw him as a traitor, a drug dealer, and a sexual pervert. Holy shit, he thought.

The officers, who were thorough, polite, and very professional, stayed an hour and left to a gang of news cameras three times the size of the one there for their arrival. They carried Cogan's desktop, his laptop, and a bag of some sort. That night and the following morning, videos and still photos of sheriff's deputies questioning Cogan were all over the national broadcast and print news. The accompanying voiceovers and headlines were similar all over the country: "Independence Advocate Quizzed About Child Porn/Drug Dealing Activities."

Cogan's phone barked off the hook. Demonstrators gathered outside his house, chanting and waving signs: *Liar*, *Phony*, *Druggie*, *Pervert*. In the middle of the night, a brick landed on his roof. He tried to get Jen to leave, but she wouldn't budge. You didn't have to take a poll to realize that less than two weeks before the election, voter support for Proposition A had gone into free fall.

Mayor Partida was floored by the Connolly allegations of the night before. The whole town was talking about it. People were outraged. Shocked. Angry. There was no way Connolly was lying. Not about something like this. Not on national television. They felt like they'd been duped. By this, this criminal. Partida suddenly understood what Ratson had been referring to. Child pornography? Drugs? God! Cogan was dead in the water. His initiative was done for. The initiative wouldn't get two percent of the vote.

CHAPTER TWENTY-THTREE

IN SHANGHAI

"I've been trying to reach you," Mattington said. "Your phones have been down."

"I needed a break from my fans," Cogan replied.

"I need to ask you some questions," Mattington said, "as soon as possible."

Thirty minutes later they met over at Boyle Park. Outside where there would be no cameras or tape recorders. Cogan wore a disguise. They sat down on a park bench. Mattington dove right in.

"I'm warning you," he frowned, "don't lead me on. If this porn stuff is true, like Connolly is saying, and if you lie to me, I'll bury you so deep in quicksand that you'll be digging yourself out in Shanghai."

"It's bullshit," Cogan answered. "All bullshit."

"Go on."

"When I launched this initiative, people warned me that powerful forces would do anything they could to discredit me, to ruin my reputation, and to defeat this measure. Ironically, one of the main things driving me in this campaign has been my fear that we can no longer trust our government. That it will stop at nothing to achieve its ends. That it will do horrible things not only to foreigners in far off countries but to U.S. citizens right here at home.

"I received an anonymous package several weeks ago. The package contained miniature cameras, recording equipment, and motion detectors, along with instructions for how to set them up so that they wouldn't be visible to intruders. The note attached to the package also gave me detailed personal information about a well-known CNN reporter—information that would give me direct access if and when the time came that I needed to contact him. The note also contained a warning about what was about to happen to me." Cogan reached in his shirt pocket and passed a portion of Giller's note to Mattington:

I have very good reason to believe that you are about to be set up by former CIA agents who are now working for that private intelligence agency we talked about. The people they answer to in D.C. have made fortunes from the cozy relationship between corrupt corporate interests and the politicians they are paying off.

You should install this equipment in your home immediately, according to the enclosed instructions. Place cameras by the front and rear doors of your house, in the hallways, in storage areas, facing your computer, in your living room, and in the bedroom. Check the cameras every night and every morning and make copies of anything critical.

If you find anything on the films, do not contact the police or any government authorities until you have gotten the information out to the public directly. The people may be one of the few things left in this country that can be trusted.

"I installed the equipment right away, and sure enough..."

"But you didn't get any pictures of their faces so how..."

"But I did. I just wanted to set Connolly up, so I didn't bring them with me." Cogan slid a set of photographs across the table. "Here they are. The top photo shows two men picking my lock and breaking into my house. The second one shows them walking up the stairs to the second floor. The third shows them working on my computer. As you can see, photo number four shows the men placing an object of some kind in a crawl space located in the hallway outside my bedroom. After seeing this one, I went to see what they had placed there. It was a large quantity of white powder that I presume to be cocaine. I replaced everything and waited to see what was going to happen. To flush them out."

Mattington studied the photos carefully. He started to chuckle.

"Does anyone know you have these pictures? Does anyone know why you had the surveillance equipment set up?"

"No."

"Holy shit. If the dots can be connected, this could really blow the roof off," he said.

"Maybe," Cogan said, "But who are these people, and how do I prove who's running this operation?"

Mattington smiled. Whatever he knew, he wasn't saying. "Can you give me the name of the guy who sent you the note and package?"

"The note wasn't signed. But I know who it was."

"Who?"

"I can't reveal that."

Mattington grunted, sweat glistening across his forehead as he shuffled through his papers.

"Have you ever heard of a guy from Houston named Bruno?"

"No."

"How about a man named Iverson?"

"No."

Mattington took out his cellphone and flashed the picture he'd taken of the two at the debate.

"Wait a second. The short one, the one on the left, I recognize his face. I remember him from the Book Depot the day that we had our organizational meeting there."

"What was he doing at the Depot?"

"He was at a table. Near where we were sitting. He had on iPod headphones. I remember because I thought it was odd. There was no iPod connected to the earphones. Just some kind of gray box. I wondered what it was. I almost asked him about it."

"Anything else?"

"Yeah, you mentioned Houston as being where this guy Bruno was from." Cogan described what little he knew about CenTel and what it was about. "I understand that CenTel is located in Houston."

"How did you learn that?"

"I can't say."

"Same reason?"

"Right."

"Interesting," sighed Mattington under his breath. He studied the photos again.

"Can I publish these?"

"That's why I'm giving them to you. But can you hold off? There's one other guy I need to talk to about this before it hits the papers."

"That's okay. I have some more work to do before this breaks."

The note in Giller's package had provided Cogan with the exact information he would need to get through. George Josephson was seated in his CNN office at the edge of the huge table when his cellphone rang. Very few people had his private cell number. He assumed it was his wife.

Tall, quick-witted, and sincere, Josephson was the perfect fresh-faced reporter to anchor CNN's news desk. Plucked a decade ago from the obscurity of KLEV in Cleveland, CNN tapped Josephson to blow through its ratings doldrums and reinstall the network at the top of the charts. Cocky and somewhat arrogant, Josephson had taken to the job like a thoroughbred to a stud farm. Within a year, he was one of the two most popular news anchors in the country.

Articulate, with teeth like piano keys and the shoulders of a swimmer, Josephson was very popular. And even though his producers disliked his independence, they were only too happy to bask in the glory of his ratings. So what if he occasionally pushed the envelope? So what if he occasionally offended the rich and powerful? That only helped boost his credibility with the average viewer. Josephson's fan base numbered in the millions and had grown steadily over the previous decade.

His reports on the big stories—tidal waves, massacres, hurricanes, bigamist enclaves, political sexploits—were legendary. He had already won every award in the field and was showing no signs of slowing down. He was smart, stubborn, tough minded, egocentric, and impossible. His detractors argued that his success was based more on personality than the quality of his reporting. But that was BS, and they knew it. He was good at what he did. Really good. And because of that, he held all the cards. Cogan was calling him from an old-fashioned, secure, pay phone.

"Josephson," he answered.

"Mr. Josephson," came the nervous reply. "I have a story I'd like to talk to you about. Is there some way we can get together?"

Reporters were used to crank calls. This sounded like one. On the other hand, how did the caller get his personal number? "Who is this?"

"I'm Sean Cogan. The guy who placed the initiative on the ballot for Fairview to declare its independence."

"I'm sorry, but that's not a story I'm going to be following," Josephson replied.

Cogan shouted: "Wait! In 1983, on March 12, you were caught by the campus police snorting cocaine with your then-girlfriend, Jessica Cooper, at West House on the Dartmouth College campus. In May 1991, you got your best friend's wife pregnant. She made up an excuse about having to attend a conference in Maryland and then had an abortion at a clinic outside of Bethesda. Your friend,

Josh Grissom, has never learned anything about it. If you'd like more, I can..."

Josephson sat bolt upright and checked around to make sure no one was within listening distance. He lowered his voice. "What do you want?"

"Listen to me," Cogan replied. "I know what you must be thinking, but I don't want anything from you. Nothing at all. I just had to get your attention. I want to give you a story with national implications. I was instructed not to use the information I just repeated to you unless something big—very big—happened, and I needed to make you realize that I was not bullshitting you. It did. That's the story I'm trying to give you. If it turns out you're not interested, fine. All I ask is that you meet with me. Privately. No third parties. No recording equipment. Just the two of us. Please, you have to believe me. This is a big deal."

"Okay," Josephson said skeptically, "we'll meet. Call me tomorrow at three and we'll set it up."

Mattington's mind was spinning. Who were the two men in the photograph he'd just been given? What was their connection to Bruno? To Ratson? Mattington needed more information. He picked up the cellphone number Bruno had given to the Hertz people. He called one mobile phone company after another. Finally, he hit pay dirt. But before driving down to the company's local storefront, he needed one more piece of information.

He placed a call to a friend who worked as a programmer for the FTC. Mattington asked how hard it would be for his friend to get Alfonse Bruno's social security number; his friend just laughed. It took less than a minute.

"This is going to sound strange," Mattington smiled to the eager sales clerk. "But I'm hoping you can help me. My briefcase was stolen from the trunk of my car. I had some really important documents in it along with my cellphone. I knew the police wouldn't have time to investigate, so rather than report them stolen, I decided to see if the thief might be dumb enough to continue using my phone. I want to try to identify the guy by finding out the calls he's placed."

"What a great idea," the clerk giggled, stepping up to a computer. She asked Mattington for his name and phone number. "Alfonse Bruno," he replied, and gave her the number. Apologizing, she asked for his Social Security number. "This is to protect your privacy," she explained. "To keep strangers from accessing your information." Within seconds Bruno's dialed numbers flashed across the screen.

"This is great," Mattington said. "Can you print this out for me?

The clerk was only too happy to oblige. "The theft of these phones is a real problem," she confided, "Go get him."

Mattington sat in his car holding his phone. The first number he called rang five times before clicking into voice mail. Mattington couldn't believe his ears.

"This is Chuck McMann," said the recording. "I'm sorry I missed your call. I am not available at this time, but your call is important to me. If you'd like to page me, hit 5 now. Otherwise please leave a detailed message, and I will get back to you as soon as I can. If you would like to send me a fax, the number is..."

Some sleuth, thought Mattington as he hung up. *Why didn't he just give callers a web address displaying his photograph and credit card numbers?*

The next number listed on Bruno's statement was answered by a sultry female voice. It belonged to Muffie, from the Oh Baby Escort Service in Houston.

The third number was answered by a live person. He uttered just two words, but that was more than enough. "Ratson here," he said, as Mattington hung up.

The fourth was Partida's office.

The fifth and sixth numbers were two more escort services.

Mattington's next call was to Partida's office. His secretary told him Partida was in a meeting.

"I'm on a deadline," replied Mattington. "Would you please interrupt the meeting?"

"I can't do that."

"Tell him it's about Ratson," Mattington insisted. "I'll hold, but I would respectfully ask that he drop whatever he's doing and take my call."

In less than ten seconds, Partida came on the line. At first he tried to bluff.

"See here," he spluttered. "Who do you think you are, calling over here and pressuring my secretary with wild stories?"

Mattington ignored him. "I suggest that you tell me what you and Ratson have been up to," he said. "Because if you don't, you'll be reading my story from your jail cell."

"Ratson?! How dare you threaten me!"

"Yes, I know all about Ratson," exaggerated Mattington. "And about Bruno and Iverson and McMann as well. You and your eat-my-hat line are in this up to your eyes. If you don't talk to me, by the time you wake up tomorrow morning you're going to wish you had."

"I don't have any idea what you're talking about. Iverson? McMann? I never heard of those people."

"Right, and you never heard of Ratson or Bruno either."

"I don't know what you're talking about. And even if I did, it would be attorney client privileged. I wouldn't be able to discuss it. Plus, there are confidentiality agreements. You're a newsman. You know about those things."

Mattington couldn't even fathom how any experienced pol—even a local hack like Partida—could possibly be such a goddamned idiot.

"I'm not going to waste any more time with you," Mattington said. "You either talk to me or I hang up. Now. If you want me to protect you as a confidential source, I'll do that. I won't quote you, and I won't identify you other than as a reliable source. If I'm subpoenaed—by anyone—I'll go to jail before I'll reveal who you are."

Partida, who had begun sweating profusely, relented. He didn't know anything about the break-in or anything like that, he said, but he would tell Mattington what he knew. Half an hour later, Mattington turned off his tape recorder, picked up the close-up photos Cogan had given him, and sat down to write his story. The next day it would be plastered all over the front pages of every newspaper in the country that carried AP stories. But first, he decided to compare notes with an old friend and colleague in the television news business.

Josephson sat in the conference room, glaring at the bean counters. The green file folder to his right held the photographs along with the notes on his discussion with Cogan. The missing part of the puzzle had just been supplied by an old friend who was an AP reporter. Other than the head of Josephson's division, the rest of the people in the room weren't even part of the news department. They were a couple of corporate bigwigs and their bifocaled buddy from legal, two money crunchers, and a mouthpiece by the name of Wadle. Wadle did all of the talking.

"If we air this story," he said, "people are going to go nuts. They will turn every sponsor against us. They will scream that it's lies, exaggeration, phony documents, a conspiracy. They will say the docs are all classified. That we are breaching national security. That this is part of a bigger picture and we can't air it without context. That we don't know what we're talking about. We need to hold off on this and get additional confirmation. We need to give this CenTel outfit a chance to respond."

"Bullshit," Josephson shot back. "I'm not holding off. This is a huge story. The docs are real, and you know it. People can respond any way they want. I'm not going to wait. Period. My source isn't some loose cannon. He's as credible as they come."

"Then why won't you tell us who he is?"

"Because I promised not to reveal his identity," snapped Josephson, "and I won't."

"Then you are forcing us into a corner. You're forcing us to kill the story, and we will," threatened Wadle.

"I won't kill it. I'll just go on camera and do the damn story. And if you pull the plug or cut me off, I'll march right out the door. And I'll take the whole damn piece right over to CBS."

"They'll throw you the hell out," Wadle said. "They'll never air it."

"Screw you. Pick up the phone and call their news director right now. Call Tom

Wilson. I anticipated this, and I've already talked to him. This story is going out. Today. If not here, then over at CBS. They have the balls to run with it if CNN doesn't. And if you kill it at CNN, you can kiss me and my ratings goodbye. Being a reporter means more to me than just filling in between toothpaste commercials. I'll jump ship. I don't want it to come to that, but I'll do it."

On that note, Josephson stood up, calmly gathered his things, and walked out of the room, leaving Wadle and the brass sitting there staring at their water glasses. Josephson had won the showdown, and everybody knew it. The second the AP story hit the wires, Josephson would be on the air with an exclusive report. That was the deal with Mattington. And Josephson intended to keep it. Nobody was going to stop him. Certainly not some bifocaled asshole with a bar card.

Before he left the room, Josephson looked back at the bean counters. "If anybody leaks a word about any of this before I go on the air, there are going to be big problems."

CHAPTER TWENTY-FOUR

ANONYMOUS SOURCES

It all hit within hours. First, Mattington's wire service article: "Establishment Attempts to Frame Independence Proponent:

"D.C. Insider Howard Ratson and Private Intelligence Outfit Work with Local Official to Destroy Critic."

Citing anonymous sources, the story described Ratson's involvement with Bruno in the anti-initiative campaign. It laid out Ratson's agenda, set forth the events that began to unfold at the Fairview High debate, and described his calls to the numbers found on Bruno's cellphone. The wire service carried the close-up photos of the two people who had broken into the Cogan home and speculated that they were acting on behalf of Ratson and Bruno. "It's only a matter of time," Mattington wrote, "before the noose tightens around all their necks. And the connection from them runs like a steel wire straight through the entire D.C. establishment." Mattington knew that readers would soon be calling to help fill in the blanks. "The fact that highly placed operatives connected through an undercover operation like this are harassing private citizens, breaking into their homes, planting criminal evidence, and seeking to destroy their lives and reputations for political gain will undoubtedly shock many Americans to the core."

Then came Josephson. "CNN has learned," he reported, "that a private intelligence organization by the name of CenTel, run out of Houston, Texas and operating with the knowledge and express approval of high-ranking leaders in Congress, has been caught breaking and entering, planting evidence, and attempting to frame Sean Cogan, a political critic who placed an independence initiative on the ballot in his small town.

"It is believed that CenTel's Director, David Henninger, personally approved the specific activities in question, which included putting child pornography on Cogan's computer, planting large amounts of cocaine in his house, setting up local law enforcement officials to obtain and serve search and arrest warrants, and conspiring with broadcasting personality Billy Bob Connolly to make false accusations against Cogan.

"Henninger is known to have close personal ties to leaders of both parties in the House and Senate. Office logs just obtained by CNN indicate that a meeting recently took place between Henninger, Washington insider Howard Ratson, and Senate Appropriations and Armed Service Committee chair, Vaughn Sawton. None were available for comment. But the office of Senator Sawton stated that he meets with lots of people every day, and he has no specific recollection of that particular appointment. CNN is following this breaking story closely. We will keep you posted."

The combined impact of the CNN and AP stories was earth shaking. The Mattington and Josephson reports soon became the topic of the day everywhere in the country. The initial reports were followed by an unrelenting twelve-hour media blood-bath the likes of which Senator Palmer Trenton, the Senate majority leader, had never seen. Both parties called emergency caucuses as they scurried for cover. No one on Capitol Hill knew how the administration was going to react, but it, too, was undoubtedly in emergency mode.

Cogan was seated at his dining room table rereading Mattington's story for the twelfth time when Mark Fischer called. He asked if they could please meet, along with the key volunteers from both of their campaigns. That came as a real surprise to Cogan. He had assumed that Katz and Fischer were both part of the Ratson, Bruno, Partida operation. Maybe not.

"I have to go back east for a few days," Sean explained. "I'm leaving in just a few hours. Jen and Geoffrey are coming with me. But go ahead and set it up with Ollie and Danielle for the day I return. Is that okay?"

"Great," Fischer said, "Okay."

Twelve days remained before the election. Invitations were now flying in from every talk-show host in the country, and Sean traveled east to campaign for a small town election. Danielle did her best to screen them and organize as many time slots as she could. The first one she wanted Cogan to do was *Face The Nation*.

"All right," said Brian Sandahl, launching into one of his trademark introductions: "Three months ago, Sean Cogan was living the private, comfortable life of a successful venture capitalist. Golfing, playing a little tennis, going to charitable events, and so on. But due to his strong feelings about some of the things he believed to be going on in this country—issues ranging from the government's taxing, spending, and deficit policies to assertions about political and corporate corruption and allegations about violations of our constitutional rights by the people sworn to protect them but acting instead in the mode of Big Brother— Cogan gave up his lifestyle to do a little tilting at windmills. He wrote an initiative that would call for his small town to form its own independent government.

"Critics accused Cogan of exaggerating the nation's problems, of being disloyal, and of doing something that was—well—crazy.

"But now, suddenly, questions are being raised about who is and isn't crazy.

"Americans are finding themselves inundated with news reports from credible sources that would seem to be substantiating just about everything Mr. Cogan has been saying about personal privacy, if not about even more. The FBI, Department of Homeland Security, National Security Agency, and CIA are all heading for the hills, and powerful members of

Congress are caucusing in secret sessions.

"And so, Mr. Cogan," Sandahl continued, "I'd like to ask you a few questions about what we might expect following this independence vote of yours. First, assuming that this initiative passes, what's going to be coming out of Fairview in terms of public policy, so to speak? What can we expect?"

Cogan wanted to avoid coming off as some kind of benevolent dictator, "Bear in mind that I can only speak for myself. We will have elections—free and fair elections, I might add—and those elected and later appointed by them will begin to devise policy."

"Fair enough," Sandahl said, "Let me ask you about your borders. Are you going to have border checks? Passports? Visas? Will vehicles have to go through some kind of checkpoint to get in?"

"I doubt it. Certainly less of a checkpoint than the one I had to go through down at the security desk in order to get upstairs to your studio."

"Good point," Sandahl smiled. "So you think that part can be worked out easily."

"Yes. Very easily."

"Okay, second, let's talk about court decisions and Supreme Court rulings. You're going to have your own courts. Correct?"

"Correct."

"On a different issue," Sandahl continued, "you've made a big point about how political payoffs, in the form of campaign contributions, have corrupted our entire system. What would you predict that Fairview is going to do about campaign contributions?"

"Ban them. And throw people who try to get around the ban in jail. Throw them in jail or," Cogan smiled, "deport them to the U.S."

"What will you do about corporate crime?"

"We will likely appoint a tough, experienced securities lawyer as our attorney general. Corporations that are stealing from stockholders, customers, or employees, that use child labor in third-world countries to manufacture their goods, or that violate environmental laws to save money will not be doing business in Fairview. It won't make any difference where they are incorporated. And we will seek to establish reciprocal treaties with other countries that do the same thing. These crooks should be prevented from selling their goods and services in law-abiding communities."

"What if Fairview goes ahead and passes your initiative, but Congress just ignores the vote?"

"If they ignore us, well, then, maybe we'll just ignore them right back."

"What do you mean by that?" Sandahl asked.

"No comment."

Sandahl smiled, pausing to let Cogan's answer sink in.

"Let's talk about taxes. Will Fairview citizens continue paying income taxes to the U.S.? "

"That remains to be seen. And it depends on how the people of Fairview vote on that issue. But it's my understanding that the people of the principality of Lichtenstein, for example, don't pay income taxes to Switzerland or Austria. I assume that the same is true for many other independent places. And now that I think about it, some of the wealthiest Americans, right here in New York, find ways to funnel money offshore and don't pay taxes to the U.S. either. So if that happens, I guess the government will have to fund its weapons of mass destructions without any more Fairview money. Besides, we might want to spend revenues for things like schools."

"What about health care?"

"I hope we'll have single-payer health care like Canada, England, France and Germany and other civilized countries."

"Who will pay for it?"

"The funds would probably come from general revenues and our savings in other areas. Plus, I imagine we might charge corporations doing business in Fairview an amount something like two-thirds of what they are already spending for employee health plans. So this would cost them less than they are now paying while providing the medical coverage people need."

"Environmental policies?"

"Again, it wouldn't be up to me. But perhaps we would sign on to many of the universally accepted protocols having to do with problems like global warming – which many special interests continue to deny. I would hope we would do whatever we can in our small way to address environmental degradation.

Nobody's going to clear-cutting our trees or drilling for oil in our parks. I can promise you that."

"One last question Mr. Cogan. Do you expect your movement to grow? Do you expect other communities across the land to follow in your footsteps?"

"I do," Cogan said. "In fact since the AP and CNN revelations we've received hundreds of emails and phone calls from people all across the country who want to join with us and start independence movements in their areas. I welcome their efforts, and we will help them in any way we can."

The highlight of Sean's East Coast media tour occurred when Jimmy Fallon asked him if he envisioned Fairview's enacting the equivalent of the Equal Rights Amendment that had failed in the U.S. years before. "Hell, yes," was Cogan's simple answer. Cameron Ryan, Fallon's main guest, had been sitting quietly next to Cogan, being her usual delicious self. She responded by shrieking, "Thank you, thank you," and jumping onto Sean's lap. With her back to the camera, she pulled up her blouse, replicating the stunt that Drew Barrymore had pulled on David Letterman for his birthday some years before. The audience went wild. Jen, who was watching from offstage, howled, and Fallon almost fell off his chair.

As soon as he returned to Fairview, Cogan called Geoffrey to find out about the meeting that Mark Fischer and Paul Katz had asked for. Cogan had no idea what to expect. None. But the group sat down with Katz and Fischer at a quiet corner table at a restaurant located some distance from Fairview. At ten in the morning, the place was practically empty.

After ordering their wake-up drinks and exchanging the stiff pleasantries of adversaries trying to be civil to one another, Fisher began. "Mr. Cogan," he said, "I speak for Mr. Katz as well as myself in saying that we owe you, Ms. Renton, Ms. Hall, Mr. Watterson, Mr. Santorum, and all of your coworkers on this initiative a big apology. We have criticized your motives, questioned your patriotism, challenged your allegations, and insulted your integrity. You were attacked, pilloried, and almost destroyed by the very forces we were so blindly defending. Mr. Katz and I had no idea about any involvement by Mr. Ratson, Mr. Bruno, or any of their people. We've been at odds with Mayor Partida from the beginning. You will, at this point, undoubtedly win this vote, and you have every right to simply toss us out the door. But where would that victory leave you? There will be legal challenges, political wrangling, more divisions, and no solutions.

"We're here to offer a proposal. This issue is now receiving nationwide and even international attention. It offers an unprecedented opportunity to bring about real change. We are absolutely appalled at what some in the leadership of Congress and the administration have done and are doing. We want nothing to do with any of it. We want change. Rectification and reform. And we want it now.

"So here is our offer: if you withdraw your initiative, authorize the town attorney to remove it from the ballot, and agree to oppose any independence efforts filed elsewhere in the country, we will agree to hold a joint press conference with you to announce that we have joined forces. Together, in a joint appeal, we will agree to three things:

"First, we would establish an independent party to field a slate of reform candidates by the next congressional elections. The primaries for those elections will be taking place in a little over seven months, and the general elections are in just a year. Members of the new party, running on a specific reform platform, will find strong support as a result of everything that has happened.

"Second, we would promote a constitutional amendment banning all financial contributions to political candidates or officeholders. Such an amendment would be a key ingredient in the campaigns of independent party candidates and would trump all existing Supreme Court decisions on the subject of campaign-finance reform. The courts could no longer hold that such reform efforts were unconstitutional because the reforms would themselves be a part of the Constitution. This would eliminate the relationship between money and politics forever.

"Third, we would join with you in calling on Congress to censure Senator Sawton. If enough members of Congress were to suddenly develop pangs of conscience about corruption and constitutional rights, we would have our vote before the next election cycle. Mr. Cogan, please do not doubt our sincerity or resolve. This needs to be done. We need to join forces and move forward, with one voice, for the good of the country. That is what we are proposing we do."

Cogan was shocked. He sat there speechless. His rabid opponents, who three days ago would have cheered if he'd been handcuffed, taken into custody, and hauled off to jail, were offering a complete about-face. The room fell silent. For minutes, the only sound was that of dishwashers noisily putting away the previous night's dinner dishes.

Finally, Cogan spoke. "Well, first," he said, "I want to thank you for your sincere apology—which we, and I think I speak for all of us, accept. I'm sure you were doing what you thought was the right thing. With respect to your suggestion about joining forces, that's intriguing. Why don't I meet with our group? I'll call you tomorrow, and we can discuss it in greater detail. Is that okay?"

"Fine, fine," replied Fischer.

"Great. We appreciate it," Katz added. "Talk to you tomorrow." Katz handed Cogan a card as they were leaving. "Call me on my cell," he said. The door closed with a pronounced thud.

As soon as they passed out of earshot, Katz turned to Fischer and grinned. "Good job," he said. "It looks like this is going to work."

Once the initiative was off the ballot and Election Day had passed, Katz and

Fischer would get into an argument with the Cogan group and with each other.

They would use the disagreement as an excuse to scuttle the whole deal.

Within months, the entire controversy that was fueling public sentiment so strongly at the moment would go away. Americans would go back to their sitcoms, and the same old forces would be back in the saddle in Washington. Different faces, different names, different costumes, but the same old deal. A few good folks would have to take the hit. That was unavoidable. Some of them might even have to retire to the Caribbean, Hawaii, or the South of France. But in no time the pieces would all be back in place.

"The King is dead," quoted Katz. "Long live the King."

After Katz and Fischer left, Cogan, Jen, Ollie, Geoffrey, and Danielle just sat there, stunned. Finally, Jen started to giggle. Pretty soon they were all laughing. Cogan grinned. "What do you want to do?"

"Are they crazy?" Geoffrey asked. "Why do they think we'd even consider it?"

"I'd rather trust a den of vipers." added Danielle.

"What do they think they're bringing to the table?" asked Sean.

"How dumb are they?" Jen laughed.

"Fuck 'em," Ollie summed up.

The decision was clear.

"Don't call them until tomorrow," suggested Jen. "Let 'em wait."

CHAPTER TWENTY-FIVE

NOVEMBER TENTH

Election Day finally arrived, and things were looking good. Yet as the hours passed, Cogan and Jen were nowhere to be seen. Nobody knew where to find them, although they were not far. They had ducked across the border to hide out in an anonymous sports-bar. Seated at a corner table, doing their best to conceal themselves, they waited patiently and strained to hear the TV commentary playing out before them. The turnout was very high—over 80%—with circling reporters appearing to outnumber voters two to one. "How did you vote? What's your take on all of this?" Most people just waved them off. The handful of locals willing to discuss their thoughts seemed sadly resigned.

As cameras surveyed the scene, Ollie's face popped up on the screen. "Mr. Waterson," urged Phil Posner of ABC, "how do you think the election is going to come out? What do you think is going to happen now?"

"I just wish it had never come to this," Ollie replied. "How did our country ever fall into the hands of these people, of these forces?"

"Do you think Proposition A is going to pass?" Posner asked.

"Seems like it will. Most people I've been talking to say they're voting for it. A lot of folks feel it's the only thing they can do."

"Congressional elections," Posner said to the camera, "will be held in just a year. The primaries are in just six months. All of the House seats and a third of the Senate will be up for grabs. There's a lot of speculation brewing about what's going to happen in those races. Do you think we're going to see much of a shakeup in Washington?"

"We probably will," Ollie said, "but it's like the old story of lipstick on a pig.

Republicans, Democrats, they all have to raise millions of dollars. It's the system that's the problem. And that's exactly the way special interests and big money want it to be. And for that reason, I think it's going to take more than a round of standard elections pitting Republicans against Democrats to solve the problem. The people are going to have to upset the whole apple cart and start all over again."

"The independence movement?"

"Right."

"What about that? ABC affiliates throughout the country are telling us that cities and towns across the country are talking about similar initiatives. Do you see this movement growing? Where is it going to wind up?"

"It's hard to say," Ollie replied. "There's the usual talk about starting a third-party movement in the hope that if enough new people were to get elected in the next go-round a year from now, then maybe the changes needed could take place. But I don't think that's realistic. The big money isn't going to let go that easily. All I know is that what has happened to America is not okay. Massive changes and reforms are needed, and it seems highly unlikely that anything of the magnitude needed could occur within the system that's in place."

Cogan and Jen sat there watching the interview. Ollie was doing a fantastic job.

"If enough people want out of the system as it's currently structured," Posner pushed, "what then? Do you see a violent movement as a possibility?"

"Absolutely not," Ollie said emphatically. "And let me add something else that's really important to understand. This movement is not about gun-waving ideologues running around ready to blow up government buildings. This is a very different situation. I don't believe it would ever come to violence. In my opinion, this is going to be resolved politically."

"But what if the other side resorts to physical force," Posner asked, "like what the National Guard did in the 60s to war protestors or with the civil rights movement, and even today? What if that happens with this, only worse?"

"Well, I just don't think it's going to come to that. "I sure hope it doesn't. But the status quo cannot continue. And it won't."

Before the votes were tabulated, exit polls confirmed that the initiative was going to pass overwhelmingly. The victory celebration that night, though Cogan refused to call it that, took place at the Fairview High School auditorium. It consisted of a brief statement by Cogan thanking the voters for passing the initiative and thanking each of the volunteers who had worked so hard on the campaign. He predicted that the independence movement would spread across the country.

"Fairview has lit the match," he said "and the flames are going to spread far and wide. They are not going to be put out by a bunch of hot air from entrenched political blowhards." With that, he was greeted by wild applause.

"In town after town, we will work with local supporters. We will make our case that there *is* something people can do. We will carry our banner: 'No more lying; no more spying; no more dying,' to the four corners of this country. The days of corruption in both the public and the private sectors are numbered. We are on the march. Fairview is on the march. Freedom is on the march. 'This land *is* your land. This land *is* my land. From California to the New York Island. From the redwood forests, to the Gulf Stream waters.' The SOBs can't have it. They can't have our freedom. We're taking it back."

The cheers were enough to trigger a seismic alert. It may not have been called a victory celebration, but it sure sounded like one. The media carried Cogan's speech across the country. Appearance requests poured in. Independence movements multiplied. It was going to become the new civil rights movement.

The independence crusade was on its way. Nobody could stop it.

Time, Newsweek, Vanity Fair. Everybody wanted interviews. They would have to wait a bit. Cogan and Jen took off. They wanted to be alone, together, before the media circus ensnared them. They climbed into Cogan's car and headed up to Skyline Drive, a beautiful road that traverses the hills above Fairview. They pulled off onto the shoulder in an area overlooking the stunning view. It was a spectacular day. They just sat there holding hands and taking in the view.

They drove all day. They visited antique shops, a deli, and a no-name grungy bar featuring torn stools and an ancient shuffleboard table. Cogan hadn't played for years. Jen had never played. Nevertheless, she beat him seven games in a row, 21-19, 21-18, 21-19, 28-26 (in overtime), 21-18, 21-17, and 21-19. Finally Cogan gave up.

"Pkaauk, pkaauk," she chided. "Big Sean's a big chicken. Pkaauk, Pkaauk."

"OK," he relented. "One more." This time she showed him no mercy and clobbered him 21 to 3. She did a little victory dance, circling him as the bartender laughed.

The road home ran south across dairy farms and open space, up through scrub hills and rolling meadows and back up to the winding turns of Panoramic Drive. The next day was going to be a busy one. Cogan's cellphone was off, but from time to time, he checked for messages.

His friend David had been oddly quiet ever since the Red Tails fundraiser at which the initiative campaign was launched. Cogan didn't know what was going on. Was he upset? Nervous? Trying to keep his distance? It wasn't like him. Suddenly a message appeared on Cogan's screen. It was from David.

"Hey Cogan. Guess you were right. Maybe this wasn't such a crazy idea after all. Give me a ring when things slow down, David. P.S. Say hi to my cousin Joe."

Joe? My cousin, Joe? Was Giller David's cousin??

Jen broke his concentration. "How do you think all of this is going to play out?" she asked.

"It's hard to tell. People are really pissed off. The child porn and planting drugs to make it look like I was trafficking really woke a lot of folks up and pushed them over the edge. Coming on the heels of all the other stuff, I think we may be in for some shocking changes. If we can keep up the pressure, I think a lot of the current batch in the House and Senate will be scrambling to save their skins. The congressional leadership will deny involvement, but all fingers are going to be pointing right at them. They'll come up with arguments to rebut everything, but the die may be cast. When all is said and done, we may actually see something along the lines of what Fischer was talking about: resignations, a campaign finance amendment to the Constitution, lots of new faces on Capitol Hill."

"Yup," Jen agreed. She sat there for a few moments.

"Sean?" she finally said.

"Yes?"

"I have a question."

"And what's that?"

"You know how you're been so adamant all along that the big money and the special interests on the one hand and the consistently distracted ambivalence of the public on the other, would make reform impossible."

"Uh-huh."

"That's what you said to all the newspaper reporters."

"Right."

"And on all the TV and radio programs."

"Right."

"At the town meeting?

"Yes."

"In the debate?"

"In the debate, yeah."

"To... well... to everybody."

"Uh-huh."

"Even to me."

"Hmmmmm."

"Well," Jen said, "it just occurred to me that if you had started out just announcing that you were going to try to reform the system, it never would have happened. It would have never gotten off the ground. There would have been little or no publicity, the public would have ignored you, and the whole thing would have just petered out like every other reform movement in history."

"Yes?"

"But what you did with this initiative movement was stir up such a gigantic ruckus that people were shaken right off of their sofas and thrown to the floor."

"Um-hum."

"And that set in motion all kinds of things."

"Like...?"

"Like Giller contacting you. Like Mattington getting interested. Like Ratson getting involved. Like CenTel breaking into your place. Like the battles with Partida and Creswell. Like the Connolly Show."

Cogan started to chuckle. Softly.

"Everybody, reporters, the voters, the volunteers... even the bad guys, just took the bait."

"The bait?"

"The bait. So, my question is: is this what you had in the back of your mind all along? Just using the independence initiative as a hook to create the kind of attention and chaos needed to completely shake things up? To shake the whole damn country awake?"

"No way."

"Are you sure?"

"Positive," Cogan replied, the slightest hint of a grin crossing his face. "And, like Groucho Marx said, 'I never tell the truth.'"

POSTSCRIPT

ayor Partida refused to return calls from the media. Reporters were out in force pressing him to make good on his promise. They sent faxes to his office, left voice mail, and badgered his doorkeeper, Laurie Feinton. They asked if he planned to add salt and pepper? Tabasco and ketchup? Onions and horseradish? Or was he just going to eat it raw? They wanted to know when it was going to happen? They wouldn't let up. And by ignoring them, he just made matters worse. The local stations had a field day, playing and replaying the tape of his promise to eat his hat if he had Cogan wrong, showing picture after picture of Partida holding his hat with the words: "Time for Dinner Mr. Mayor" written across the screen. One station ran an editorial cartoon depicting a scowling Partida seated at his desk with the caption: "The hat stops here."

Following an unpleasant interrogation by his producers and an email from Sadie that proclaimed "Screw you, pin dick. I quit," Billy Bob Connolly decided to take an extended sabbatical in a remote region of County Cork in western Ireland. Someplace where maybe he could avoid satellite dishes, cable hookups, and even televisions. Last seen, he was holding court at O'Reilly's Pub and Bath reciting poetry, singing Irish folk songs, and learning to play the accordion.

Joseph Giller, still mysterious, simply vanished. Cogan worried that perhaps he had been taken in, grilled, and God knows what else. But then Giller's familiar voice suddenly turned up as a message on Cogan's new, unlisted, cellphone.

"Hey! How's it going? Glad you were able to hook up the cameras without electrocuting yourself. Hi to my cousin." There was no explanation. And no return number. He had to have a conversation with David soon.

Then, one day out of the blue, after he forgotten about the bet, Cogan received an envelope with a PO Box as the return address. In it sat a hundred-dollar check made out to Planned Parenthood with a note that read: "A deal is a deal. You may hate me and the things I believe, but at least you know I'm a man of my word. Good luck. Faithfully yours, Moe-zus"

Cogan grabbed a pen and wrote back: "Dear Moe-zus. Thank you. But believe it or not I would never want you to do something against your beliefs—not even on a bet. I will take care of the check to Planned Parenthood myself, and I am returning yours. Hopefully, someday we will both realize that despite our sharp differences, you and I have more in common than we think. We both want the best for the world, and we both want to live in a place that values and honors freedom. That includes, of course, freedom of religion. Pray for me. I will need that in the months ahead. God bless you, Sean."

Ray Bourhis is uniquely qualified to be a political pundit and an enemy of unbridled corporate and political corruption. A lawyer practicing out of San Francisco and Rancho Santa Fe, California, Bourhis has been at the forefront of the battle against greed and excessive power for most of his life.

Bourhis grew up in the tough neighborhood of Elmhurst in Queens, New York. He credits an attempt by local street gang members to throw him, at the age of twelve, into a blazing

bonfire with helping him develop the survival skills needed to spend his legal career taking on insurance companies.

Bourhis got his BA at Ohio State University.

After graduating from Ohio State, he took a job teaching in a rural high school in Appalachia, where he got fired for putting together a pilot project with Senator Robert Kennedy for students to work on Arizona Indian Reservations during the summer. Bourhis wound up as one of Kennedy's key staffers, working with the

Senator on his presidential campaign. He then joined the Domestic Peace Corps (VISTA) and was sent to California as a community organizer with the farm workers. Ray's passion for fighting for the underdog ultimately led him to the UC Berkeley School of Law where he founded a student-run public interest law firm that became known as CalPirg. He proceeded to go toe to toe with Ronald Reagan appointees Ed Meese and William French Smith.

Bourhis' ***Revolt*** reflects a lifetime of distain for what he considers the hijacking of America by special interests. He believes that the events portrayed in Revolt may well come to pass turning fiction into fact.

In addition to ***Revolt***, Bourhis is the author of Insult to Injury, Autobiography of Brutus Buckeye, and This Ain't Harvard. The father of four children, he lives in Rancho Santa Fe, California.

www.ingramcontent.com/pod-product-compliance
Lightning Source LLC
Chambersburg PA
CBHW051236130726
47988CB00001B/371